HOPPER GRASS

HOPPER GRASS

CHRIS CARLTON BROWN

HENRY HOLT AND COMPANY
NEW YORK

Henry Holt and Company, LLC
Publishers since 1866
175 Fifth Avenue
New York, New York 10010
www.HenryHoltKids.com

Library of Congress Cataloging-in-Publication Data
Brown, Chris Carlton.
Hoppergrass / Chris Carlton Brown.—1st ed.
p.   cm.
Summary: In a Virginia juvenile detention center, intelligent, well-bred
Bowser relates his incarceration as "a victim of circumstances" and his
unlikely friendship with Nose, an African American with a story to tell.
ISBN-13: 978-0-8050-8879-3
ISBN-10: 0-8050-8879-2
[1. Juvenile detention homes—Fiction.   2. Conduct of life—Fiction.
3. Race relations—Fiction.   4. Virginia—Fiction.]   I. Title.
PZ7.B812857Hop 2009   [Fic]—dc22   2008040603

First Edition—2009
Designed by Patrick Collins / Hand lettering by Jessica Hische
Printed in the United States of America on acid-free paper. ∞

1 3 5 7 9 10 8 6 4 2

To Caleb

HOPPER GRASS

HOW TO USE THE COMMODE

IT'S ALWAYS A CLEAN white car—this time a Ford. It's always a young man who drives it, a student of social work or corrections. Cornfields and pastures roll on the opposite side of the glass like a movie until we get to the river and cross it. When we arrive at the Intake Cottage, I sit on an orange plastic chair in front of two ladies who are typing. One of the ladies makes a call, and after a while, a skinny man comes in. The lady hands him a file, and the driver hands me over to the skinny man, who takes me to a room with more plastic chairs around a table. One boy with a buzz cut, wearing brown clothes that remind me of grocery bags, sits at the table. We can hear the ladies through the wall, typing and chatting.

As soon as the skinny man leaves, the other boy starts to talk. "My name's Beadron. They call me

Babybird. On the street, I was the singer for a band. You ever heard of the Sheba Club in DC?" I shake my head. "We played there," he says. Then he half closes his eyes and starts to sing, "I won't be your second choice. I'm going to be your number one or I'm not going to be there at all." He sings it too slowly, so I don't recognize the song until later. He really looks like a baby bird. His neck's long, and his head is fuzzy.

After a while, a man comes in and calls my name from the open file folder in his hand. He is very big and half bald and speaks in a no-nonsense but relaxed deep voice. "My name is Mr. Ball. I'm going to take you up to Cottage B." Then he walks me up the hill in the June heat. A breeze blows now and then off the river that spreads below and behind us. Boys in the distance are cutting grass with sickles.

On the hill, a big old brick dining hall spreads across one end of the courtyard. At the opposite end there's another building, not as wide but high, that looks like a huge brick barn. Next to the brick barn is a white chapel. Old brick cottages flank the other two sides of the courtyard, and sycamores line the sidewalks. If you could shrink the courtyard, it would look like a model "hometown of the past" on a train set. We head off down behind Cottage B, on the far side of the square next to the brick barn.

Down the slope, you can see cows in the fields

and a barn in the distance. Closer in to the cottage, boys with buzz cuts and grocery-bag uniforms and brogues are beginning to stand up from the shade of live oaks. They are lining up for watermelons that are quartered and handed out from the back of a flatbed truck. Boys are sitting around in clusters under the oaks in the still afternoon heat, chattering and eating watermelon, with that breeze now and then coming up across the fields from the river.

Mr. Ball took me over to Mr. Lindquist, the Cottage B housefather. Mr. Lindquist was thin and not tall, but he spoke hearty. "Welcome to Belmont School for Boys," he said. He told me he was a marine and that the boys of Cottage B were good boys, mostly, but if I had any trouble, I was to tell him and not try to settle it myself. "If there's going to be any fighting around here, it's going to be with me." Then he told me to get in line for some watermelon before it was all gone. I was the only one in line wearing street clothes.

I got a quarter of a watermelon and went over and sat next to two white boys under a tree. A dark-haired boy with freckles asked me, "Did you come up from the Diagnostic Center?"

"Yeah," I said.

"I'm Evan. What's your name?"

"Bowser."

"That's a dog's name," said Evan.

A big boy with wiry blond hair broke in, "You call him a dog, he'll show you to a dog named Duke, man. I was at the Diagnostic Center with this boy. He got into it with a big black guy and shot his cuff—got him right by his trousers and threw him. He'll give you a go with the dukes all right."

"We call him Snicklesnort," said the freckled boy.

"Snicklesnort? Is that what they called you at the Diagnostic Center?" I asked him.

"No, they called me Jerry." I could see how he got his nickname. He talked as though he were complaining all the time.

"Yeah, I remember you at the Diagnostic Center," I said. It wasn't true, but as soon as I said it, it became part of our story; we knew each other before we got to the Hill.

At the Diagnostic Center the boys thought I might be squirrelly because I was quiet and read books. We had wrestling one day, and I pinned a hardrock who didn't know how to wrestle. That I didn't get creamed surprised everyone so much that stories started popping up in other cottages. Sometimes I beat up a big guy, sometimes two, sometimes a counselor. I figured it was a good story to keep me out of fights. Each boy who told it knew it would put him on my good side, and it did.

All the boys went through the Diagnostic Center: deaf boys, retarded boys, abused boys, insane boys, delinquents, and boys who didn't have anywhere else to go. All the girls went through the Diagnostic Center too, but lived in separate cottages. We were all sorted and distributed out from there. Boys were sent to foster homes or to forestry camp or to special treatment schools. Delinquent boys fourteen and older came to Belmont School for Boys, known to us as the Hill.

There were twenty of us in Cottage B. Mr. Lindquist and his wife lived in the part upstairs that looked like a house. Before breakfast and after dinner we hung out in the cottage basement and Mr. Lindquist watched us from a desk in front. We sat on indestructible wooden chairs, which were painted with thick enamel the gray color of a ship's hull, at heavy round wooden tables that would be nearly impossible to throw and would be hard to even turn over. The tables were enameled the same forest green as paint that covered the cinderblock walls up to chest height from the concrete floor. After showers, we marched upstairs to a dorm wing where we slept in double-decker bunks stacked along both walls of a narrow hall, with windows at intervals on each wall. They left the windows open, so you could hear night insects through the security mesh.

That first evening, I took a seat at the table with Snicklesnort, Evan, and Babybird. There was also a Mexican kid there named Ben Susan. Evan introduced him. "You heard of the boy named Sue? This is the girl named Sue."

5

Ben Susan gave him a dark look, and Evan laughed and patted him on the shoulder. "Ben Susan's a good guy." The Mexican was small, but he was sprung tight like a switchblade.

We started swapping stories right off, Hill stories and street stories. Babybird was talking about how he got sent up. "My uncle and me was breaking into soda and snack machines all over the county. When my uncle went to court, the judge said, 'Six months in the county jail,' and my uncle said, 'I can take that standing on my head.' So the judge said, 'All right. One to three years, state penitentiary.'"

Babybird was chuckling over how witty his uncle was until Snicklesnort weighed in. "That is the stupidest thing I have ever heard."

Babybird snapped back at him, "I'll tell you what: My uncle can kick your ass." Then he settled back, satisfied that he'd won the argument.

Babybird turned to me. "You're going to need a locker mate. You want to share with me?"

"Sure," I said without thinking, and everyone went quiet for a minute, like I'd farted.

When I got up to go to the water fountain, Ben Susan got up too. I didn't like him walking behind me, so I stopped and turned aside and he stopped too.

Mr. Lindquist yelled, "Smoke 'em if you got 'em."

Ben Susan said, "Shoot me a fog," and I took out a

Camel for him and one for me. We were standing at the entrance to the area with sinks and showers. "Listen, man," Ben Susan said, "you don't want to share your locker with Babybird. He don't get nothing from home. He'll be smoking all your fogs. Pair up with Evan; he gets cookies and stuff all the time."

Back at the table, Babybird had picked up a pencil and was drawing pictures. Snicklesnort asked me what I was sent up for, and I answered, "Nothing."

"Nothing?" he asked.

"Yeah. I was a victim of circumstance," I said.

They all stared at me, trying to figure out whether I was messing with them. The answer had already become an inside joke between me and myself. I knew I was guilty as hell. I just couldn't come up with the right story of exactly what it was I was guilty of. What I knew for sure was that Bradley Davis was dead, and that if there were any circumstances to blame, I wasn't a victim of them—I had made them. The answer always distanced me from the other boys.

"How about you, Evan?" I asked.

"Dope," Evan said, and told the story.

I got a coffee can full of mescaline powder, and I was capping it and selling it at school. One day I took the can and the empty caps and put them in my locker.

Somebody ratted on me, and they busted my locker open with a crowbar. There was some pot in there, too. The vice principal came with two cops to get me in the gym. I went along with them, saying, "Surely, officers, there must be some mistake," until we got outside. When we got halfway to the cop car, I squatted down like I was sick.

One of the cops leaned over me and asked, "Are you on drugs right now, son?"

I nodded, holding my belly, then bolted right under his arm, yelling, "But I can still outrun your sorry ass." I was hauling with both cops behind me, feeling the traction of my Joe Lapchick ground grabbers, and yelling to my bobos "Don't fail me now, Joe!" When I got to the woods behind the school, I dived into a bush and peeked out to see 'em go past. Then I doubled back and just strolled over to my friend's car and lay down in the back seat looking at a *Playboy* until he came out.

When he saw me, he cracked up laughing and said, "I guess you better stay in my barn tonight." For three weeks, I hung around town and played track and field with the cops. During the day, I went fishing or swimming at the river. I went alone mostly, but sometimes a friend would skip school and go with me and we'd blow a joint. After school, girls would bring me fried chicken and potato salad and stuff from home, and I'd play sandlot football or hang out at the Pizza Box. But I always stayed outside so I could run, and I always wore my Joe Lapchick ground grabbers.

About twice a week a cop would spot me and yell, "Collar that boy!"

I'd take off running with two or three cops after me, yelling, "Don't fail me now, Joe." Every time I'd outrun them until I got to a bush and I'd dive in. When they started looking around for me, I'd bolt off in a different direction, then I'd stroll back to the gang like nothing happened and the crowd would go wild.

Babybird's drawing looked like a Road Runner cartoon. Evan's feet were giant sneakers, and they were making circles to show how fast he was going, bolting away from a bush. A Wile E. Coyote in a cop uniform was holding a club up in the air with his nose stuck in the bush. The caption read, *"Evan says: 'Joe Lapchick's ground grabbers is faster than cops.'* I thought the cartoon was good and passed it on to Snickle.

"How'd they finally nab you?" I asked Evan.

I was fishing at the river. It was a nice spring day, and I thought I'd blow a joint. I fell asleep for a while, and when I woke up, I heard them little Hostess white powdered doughnuts at the 7-Eleven calling for me. "Come eat me, Evan. Come eat me." And I rose up blood-shot like a zombie and followed the voices right up the

9

path and up the street and into that damned 7-Eleven and to that doughnut shelf and I found that pack that was calling for me and started shoving him in my mouth. The guy behind the counter looked like Bela Lugosi, and he was always chatting it up with the cops. I saw Bela jumping up and down like a cheerleader when he saw them coming, but instead of running, I just kept eating with one hand and shoving them little white doughnut packs in my pockets with the other.

"Where'd all this happen?" I asked.

"Fredericksburg."

"You got a locker mate?" I asked Evan. He shook his head. I said, "I'll locker with you." Then I turned to Babybird. "Sorry, man." Babybird waved it off. We both knew that the other guys had already decided who was going to be my locker mate. They just hadn't told Babybird. Maybe they didn't even have to tell one another; it was just the right order of things.

Every morning we'd go down to the dining hall and stand in a long line in the courtyard. You had to keep your hands in your back pockets, and there was no talking in line. The hall was like a gigantic brick cave with slow fans hanging down from a ceiling that seemed fifty feet high. I wouldn't be surprised if the hall had been there in the Civil War. The whole place smelled as though past meals cooking had worn into the bricks. It was nice, like the taste of tobacco in a pipe after the bowl is cured.

Boys in worn white outfits, with white hats the shape of coffee cans, served up the food. Since you had your hands in your back pockets and couldn't talk, you'd nod your head at what you wanted, and they'd slap it on your plate and pass it down on your tray. The food was more than okay, although you'd never catch a boy admitting it. It was good, fresh food grown right there on the farm, grown and slaughtered and prepared by the boys themselves. It was farm food—they didn't waste much of anything—but I got so I would even shovel away cow's brains on toast and like it.

During my first breakfast there, Babybird told me the cooks beat off in the liver. You could see the huge open kitchen from the front of the dining hall, and it was hard to picture how the cooks could pull it off. But every boy on the Hill believed that the cooks beat off in the liver, even if they didn't think it really happened, and no boy ever ate the stuff. That didn't keep them from serving it, though. About once a month they'd serve liver, no one would eat it, and I guess they threw it all in with the hog slop or something.

After breakfast they marched us out into the courtyard by cottages. Then they called groups out for jobs or school. The first detail they called out was

11

special force. For your first two weeks they put you on special force with rehab lab and orientation.

I didn't have any idea what I was supposed to do, but Snicklesnort motioned me to fall out and kept a close watch on me from the first. Snickle was the only boy who did special force all the time as a regular job. He did whatever the crew boss told him. All the boys called the crew boss Shorty Nub when he couldn't hear them. I never knew his real name until much later. Shorty Nub always called Snickle "Side" as in "sidekick." And he liked to deliver his orders through Snickle rather than directly to the boys, even if the boys could hear him giving the orders. He'd say, "Side, go tell that towheaded runt that if he don't pick up his pace he could be working through lunch without no water." The blond boy could hear the Nub's voice— lazy, like a banjo played out of tune on purpose just to annoy you—but Snickle would still have to come over and say to the boy, "Boss says pick it up."

It was the end of June and hot as hell. They didn't load us up in the trucks or anything, they just gave us hand sickles and told us to get on our hands and knees and cut grass around the hedges. We were hot and thirsty and bored, but the worst part was know- ing that we were doing nothing—that they could do the work we were doing with a tractor.

Around eleven o'clock, I got a big blister on my hand and it broke. Snickle had run to do an errand. I thought the Nub might take me out of the sun to get a bandage. He was black and stout with green eyes that locked on you as though he were staring you down all the time and was always just about to lash out. All the boys were afraid of him, but word was he was even tougher on the black boys than the whites. He listened to country music, and boys said he wanted to be just like a white redneck, like Charley Pride, and he was pretty good at it. He managed to keep his hair cut in the shape of a box, the shape of a white man's hair greased back, with sideburns that got broader below the ears.

I walked up to Shorty Nub and showed him my hand. "Sir, I can't sickle anymore with this hand. May I go to the infirmary to get it taped up?"

Shorty Nub locked on me fearsome and asked, "How many hands you got, boy?"

"Two, sir," I answered.

"Let me see them," Shorty Nub said. I held both hands out to him, palms up.

Shorty Nub said, "That other one don't look blistered." I didn't quite get his meaning, so I stood there looking at him with my hands out. "What the hell are you looking at?" he asked me. I felt like saying, "Not much," but his green eyes were locked on me, and I figured this might not be a good time to get sassy. "You supposed to be some kind of Einstein, ain't you?" he asked.

13

"Sir?"

"Sir?" he mocked back at me.

"You supposed to be 'highly intelligent,'" he sneered. "Well this week you ain't going to study nothing but sickles and grass, you understand me? Now get back there and cut some grass with your left hand. When that gets blistered, use your teeth."

After Snickle got back, he took the first opportunity to get near enough to me to whisper, "Homeboy, listen careful: If you need anything, you ask me. Never let the Nub know you want something." It was lucky having Snickle be from my table. He knew what he was talking about.

Whenever a boy asked for water, the Nub would just glare at him, then call Snickle over and tell him to keep that boy working during the next water break. Even if somebody needed to pee, they had to ask Snickle.

If you got in trouble after your first two weeks, they'd throw you back on special force for punishment. Naturally, with Shorty Nub in charge, the new boys on force liked to get pulled out to rehab lab, even though you spent most of your time there sitting on plastic chairs waiting to take tests.

When they call you out for orientation, they mostly buzz-cut your head and they fit your brogues and your uniform and tell you some rules. Most of what you need to know, though, they don't tell you. They tell you how to pull your sheets tight around your bunk hospital-style when you get up in the morning and do it fast if you don't want to get kicked by the morning man. But they don't tell you how to dance around the other guys near you to do it. You're all in your underwear, so if you rub somebody wrong, you're going to have to fight. On the other hand, if you stand back and give way too much you'll have to fight or be a punk sooner or later. How to stay out of fights without getting pegged a punk is something you learned by experience. If you were lucky, you could get some help from a homeboy, but I generally kept to myself.

Before showers that first night on force I learned about how to use the commode. The commodes are all lined up against a wall in the cottage basement, out in the open with no walls between them. I looked at them and figured I'd forget everyone else and act natural. It turns out that you've got to take special care to keep your ass flat down on the seat and lift as little as possible to wipe yourself or to slip your pants back up. I was standing, pulling my pants up, and a black kid called Nose was sitting on the commode next to me. I heard another black boy named Gray yell out, "Look at that boy wipe his white ass right there in your face."

I started to walk out of the commode area when I

felt a slap on the back of my head. I turned around to see Nose squared off. He was shorter than me, and his nose was flattened sideways against his cheek. It looked like it had been broken at some time and never set. "You shove your ass in my face," he said, "I'm going to kick it."

I'd seen this routine before, at the county jail and at the Diagnostic Center, but I'd never had to play along until now. "I can stand for it," I said.

And Nose: "You can lay for it, punk."

And me: "You see a punk, smack him."

Nose walked backward the few paces to the shower area, motioning me to come after him the way you'd direct a truck backing up.

There was one bulb hanging outside the shower, and it lit a fighting pit in a fifteen-by-twenty-foot space. The bloods fought in a different way. I'd seen them, but I'd never fought one before. They hold both dukes forward and jump in and out like a kangaroo. This wasn't like fighting on the street. There was no sense trying to box and wear the guy out. I knew word would spread, and as soon as the boys started streaming in to watch, Mr. Lindquist would bust through and break up the fight.

I lunged at Nose with a sucker punch, stayed in close, and got him against the wall. Then I kept the short punches going like a jackhammer, left to the head, right to the head, left to the head, right, and a right to the body. When he started to counterpunch, I jumped way back and crouched, blocking. He jumped once into me and hit hard twice, once to the left side of my head, which I blocked, and once hard into my right side, which made me buckle.

We heard Mr. Lindquist's voice over everything: "You fight somebody, you fight me." Mr. Lindquist was in Nose's face. I could see that Nose was pumping and he was about to lay into Mr. Lindquist, so I yelled, "I started it." Then Mr. Lindquist was in my face.

"You're here less than a week and you're already stirring up a fight?" I could tell that Mr. Lindquist had not wanted to fight Nose, but he was on me now and couldn't back down. "Bowser, you fight anyone, you fight me. You fight me, I'll kick your ass. If I don't kick your ass, I'll get you; if I have to take a tire iron to your head while you're asleep, I'll get you. Do you understand me?"

I could see that he was being a marine and he was probably doing something he had been trained to do. You could almost hear the air come out of the fight when I stood to attention and said, "Yes, sir."

That was the first scrap I'd actually had in the joint. But in a way it seemed familiar. As far back as I could remember I had trouble getting the rules straight and then had to fight about it. After the fight, there were always stories: The kids would tell them, or their parents would tell them, or the teachers would tell them. Sometimes the police would tell them, and sometimes they told them in court.

The worst part was the stories I told myself. In here there wasn't any hooch or weed or pills to slow them down. "I was stoned" is a lousy excuse, but it's simple.

Anyway, after that scrap I'd walk a long way around to avoid Nose. Since he was black, it didn't seem it should be that hard, but it was.

HILL TIME STORY TIME

YOU FELL PRETTY QUICKLY into who sat at what table. There were two tables with all white boys and two tables with all black boys. Being the only Mexican in the cottage, Ben Susan could sit at a white or a black table if he wanted to. I stuck with the boys I started with: Babybird, Snicklesnort, Ben Susan, and Evan, my locker mate. The lockers aren't divided very well. You both put stuff in the locker, and once it's there either one of you can take it out. You'd think that locker mates would squabble about who put in more or who took out more, but they never did.

I guess Evan got an okay deal. I took up a lot of locker space with at least two books at a time and one or two notebooks. But on the plus side, my family sent me enough goodies and cigarettes for both of us, and I always had money for canteen. Evan always kept the same truck in the locker: white powdered doughnuts, a carton of Marlboros, a shoe box, a picture album with a photo of the Eiffel Tower on the cover, and a radio/cassette player. He kept letters from home in the shoe box and a few cassette tapes from his sister. He used the radio/cassette player to play tapes from home and to record tapes to send back.

About a week after I'd gotten off force, after dinner and before showers, we were sitting around the table smoking. All of the boys at all of the tables were smoking and talking. Snicklesnort had to yell above the noise in the cottage basement. He took a drag and leaned into the smoke above the table. "Shorty Nub got smoked up today, boy. I'm telling you, he was drunk." We all leaned in with our arms crossed in front of the aluminum foil ashtrays as though we were playing cards. Snickle launched into the story.

———

Yeah, man, special force was throwing up hay, and Mr. Greenjeans dropped by the barn in that piece-of-trash pickup. Y'all know Mr. Greenjeans? You always see him around here painting or fixing a roof or something. He looks a lot like Shorty Nub, except he's white and wears overalls.

So anyway, the Nub left me in charge and walked down to the drive. I told the boys, "If you're thinking about running, you go ahead. You won't get as far as the woods. Even if you do, those dogs'll get you and the Nub will be whaling on you before morning."

Shorty Nub came back after a few minutes and said to all the boys, "I got to go down the street and get some supplies. Side here is in charge, and I swear I will beat anyone he says went outta line. You all hear me?"

There ain't a clock up there, but I reckon it was about one thirty when he left. In about two hours we had thrown up all the bales, even though nobody was busting hump. So everybody was just lounging around on hay bales. I got a fog from a new boy and went outside to smoke it.

When I came back in, I looked around and two of the boys were gone. When he saw the look on my face, one of the boys said, "Nobody ran. Specter just took Shirley Prince back in the stable."

When I came up on them, they were laying back together on some hay bales. Shirley Prince's hand was on Specter's pant leg.

I said, "What do you think you're doing?"

Specter said, "Shirley Prince is my gal, ain't you, Shirley?"

Shirley was steaming. "The hell I am," he said, "You keep calling me that and I'll kick your ass. I'm your WOMAN!"

So I said, "You ain't no boy, girl, man, nor woman. You a damned IPHODITE! And if the Nub finds out about this, they sure going to shoot you a six."

Just then it seemed like the whole barn smelled like a still. I looked around and Shorty Nub was coming around the corner stumbling drunk. He was wobbling, and he was yelling about "abonimation."

"Damn queers. This is an abonimation in the eyes of the Lord!" Then he started lurching toward us while trying to get his belt off.

So I'm going, "What the hell is this? The Nub wants to get it on with Shirley Prince?"

Then Shorty Nub said to me, "Hold that black queer bastard down and I'll strop him." He pulled his belt free so hard that it spun him around like a top and he fell flat on his face.

We were all hooting and howling at this point until Mr. Lindquist had to yell at us to keep it down. We leaned in closer for Snickle to finish the story.

After that I had to check the time on the Nub's watch to see when we had to rouse him for supper. Each time I said, "I needs a damn gas mask. These cheap hooch fumes is goin' to kill me." When it was time to go, it took us fifteen minutes to rouse him, and he was still so smoked up I thought he was going to run the truck into a ditch.

At the end of Snicklesnort's story, there was a lag in the conversation, but everything beyond the five of us at the round table was white noise.

Babybird said, "When I get out of here, I'm going to get my band back together, and we'll move to DC and play the Sheba Club."

Snicklesnort shot that one down. "Yeah, when you move to DC, you send me a postcard."

I started the patter up again. "When I get out of here, I'm going to get a motorcycle." I could picture myself moving, moving and alone and outside.

Evan said, "Yeah, me too."

Babybird said, "Yeah, we'll all get motorcycles and travel all over the country together."

Evan said, "We can go to Mexico and buy pot and bring it back."

Ben Susan's voice was high but loud. "I will go with you." Several boys were ready to jump in with the next piece of the story, but Ben Susan shouted them down. "I will go with you to Mexico, and we will get the pot. And you will travel with me to find my mother."

We talked about fighting or boys getting beaten by the man all the time, but fights and beatings didn't happen very often and they weren't what made life on the Hill hard. In fact, I think boys fought and got in trouble mostly for relief. We always talked about big things we were going to do together when we got out, but we knew that we would probably never see one another again. We had been pulled out of real life, and we were no longer real ourselves. It made time seem as though it went on forever without meaning anything.

I got to think of there being two times: Hill time and story time. You measure Hill time in progress. At Belmont you come up for progress after your first six months. At progress, a counselor reviews your file and tells you what a committee decided about how many months to the next progress. If you're good, they shoot you a three, if you're bad, they shoot you a six. You want a three because there's a chance that they'll tell you next time, "You're doing well. Keep it up and we may give you a release date on your next progress." Hill time is about when it will end.

You don't measure story time at all. It's like the time in a dream. Something in story time isn't true because it happened or even could happen. It's true because you wish it had happened, or wish it will happen, or wish it could happen.

When it came time for showers, I did my best to stay clear of Nose. Gray was the guy who handed out the clean laundry before showers. He was a bodybuilder and looked half white and maybe part Indian, but he was counted black. He always seemed amused by whatever was going on. When you got your pile of laundry, you took out everything but your underpants, your undershirt, and your towel, and put them in your locker. Then you took your towel and underwear and laid them over a waist-high block wall outside the shower stall. When you got out of the shower, you grabbed the towel marked with your name, then put on the underpants and undershirt with your name, then lined up in your underwear to get into the bunkroom.

I was dreaming story time in the shower: I was on a motorcycle and I was moving, but I didn't picture anywhere I was going. It was like moving was a place where I could live and I could stay there and be satisfied. And everybody anywhere I traveled knew me by name and called me Captain Grover. And everybody knew that I would protect them if anyone was cruel to them. I came out of the shower and grabbed what I thought were my briefs, but I was dreaming and didn't check the name. When Nose came out of the shower, he looked on the wall where his underwear had been. As I turned, I saw his face as he realized that I had taken his, and his look was so hard it jerked me back.

I was in a double-file line wearing nothing but Nose's underwear when I realized what I'd done and started to remove the underpants slowly, trying, somehow, to be cool. I heard Gray say, "That boy got your damn underpants," and I could see boys roiling for a fight, the way fish roil when you throw bread on the water.

One of the black boys said, "Bowser don't just be putting his ass in Nose's face. He got to be wearing his damn shorts." All of the boys were standing around in their underwear, staring and excited.

Nose held up my underpants, and he glanced around at the brothers. Then he regarded my briefs for a moment, reached over and grabbed my undershirt and towel, and walked over to me. I was standing naked in line, trying to look fierce while holding Nose's underwear out to him. He looked straight in my eyes with his nose flattened against his face, so calm I thought that he was trying to ease down my guard. Then his mouth broadened into a huge smile that showed all his teeth. I drew back.

Nose's smile disappeared. He grabbed his clothes from out of my hand, and still staring straight into my eyes, he dropped my clothes on the floor in front of me. I would have had to hit him, but Mr. Lindquist pushed through the crowd and kept us apart until we got to our bunks.

I guess Nose and I facing off, stark naked, in a steamy room full of boys, captured boys' imaginations. From that time on, everyone believed that one of us was going to kill the other. It was like believing the cooks beat off in the liver. It made good story. We were a pretty even match and he was a black kid from the slums and I was a white kid from a nice neighborhood. The story spread all over the Hill, and as the story got stoked, Nose's and my characters got stoked too, until we sounded like pro wrestlers or like superheroes in a comic book.

Nose was the most dangerous street fighter who ever lived. He brought down a whole Mafia gang that was crowding his turf. Then he killed twenty cops before they could bring him in. People started calling me Professor and said I got kung fu secrets out of all the books I read and studied with a grand master.

You'd hear things like, "Nose going to send Professor back to school. Professor can read all the books he wants, but the Nose knows! Nose going to mess him up, man. You wait and see."

Or, "Nose is the scrapper, all right. He'll shoot a man's cuff before he sees him coming, but that ain't no match for the secret knowledge."

I got a big kick out of this whole performance, and I think Nose did too. I started acting along when people talked to me about "the Grudge Match." At canteen a skinny black boy from another cottage said, "Hey, Professor, show me a karate chop."

"What I know, I know," I told him. "There is no need to prove my knowledge to others."

Another time, a white boy from the country asked, "Professor, when are you going to mix it up with that Nose boy? You don't want people to think you're chicken, do you? Are you going to call him out or just smack him upside the head?"

I answered, "The superior man abhors violence. Nevertheless, there comes a time when a man must stand for what is right."

Nose was acting along, too. You could tell by his walk. He started doing this thing where he'd lean to his left on a long stride with his right foot, then hop up quick with his left, so you could almost hear funky drums when you saw him coming. And when people asked him about the Grudge Match, he was coming up with some good gangster lines like "The Nose is rough and the Nose is tough, but the Nose ain't never mean." Some of the lines that worked best were rhymes where you couldn't figure out exactly what he meant, like "You know what the man say, bro, 'Yo bet yo money on Charlie Chin, yo bet enough yo sho to win. Right on!'" Boys didn't want to admit they didn't know what it meant, so they'd remember it and pass it on, hoping another boy would shed some light on it.

I was having a great time, mostly thanks to Evan. My whole character came from him. He started all the rumors about me and the secret knowledge. Come to think of it, I think Evan cooked up the whole Grudge Match from scratch. At night, he'd coach me on my character, and he'd tell all the other boys at the table what to say if anyone was to ask them about me and the fight. If anyone asked if I really had secret knowledge, Evan told them they must say, "All I can tell you is this, my friend: The fight will be over before the first punch is thrown."

Miles seemed to be Nose's coach. Sometimes I would see him taking Evan aside for a talk. To this day, I don't know whether Miles was putting Evan up to putting me up or whether Evan was putting Miles up to putting Nose up. Anyway, Evan told Babybird he should draw pictures and pass them around. Every day Babybird would come up with a new one, and each one was better than the last.

One day he drew a picture of Nose facing off against a motley gang of hoods in an alley between tall buildings. The hoods were leering and ugly, wielding switchblades and chains. Nose was shirtless and bulging with ridiculous muscles, with a rag tied around his forehead and a trash can lid in his left hand like a shield and a gigantic switchblade in his right hand like a sword. The caption read, "Street Power: The Nose Knows."

The next day, he did a drawing of me sitting in a lotus position in a Chinese robe with my eyes closed. In the picture, I am holding out my right hand and lightning is flashing from my palm to knock the pistol out of the hand of a startled thug. The caption read, "The Professor will kung fu you." Then he drew a series of pictures of us facing off, all with the same caption: "Who will be left standing?"

Evan told me to get a yoga book out of the library. I brought it to him, and he started picking out strange-looking positions and laughing. He marked several that he said I must do every morning outside the shower so everyone could see me. Every morning, I would sit in a full lotus, and as people came by, I would make weird sounds and move to standing on my head and into other contortions from the book.

I started calling Evan my mouthpiece. Sometimes we would take his boogie box under the stairs and listen to music and conspire about the Grudge Match, or tell stories from the street or stories about what we were going to do when we got out. Back at the table, Snicklesnort was mostly grumpy on everything. "Who ever heard of 'secret knowledge'?" he'd ask. Or he'd just say, "Get out of here with that stuff!" But sometimes he'd pitch right in with a line for our script or an idea for Babybird to draw. Snicklesnort, Evan, Babybird, Ben Susan, and I shared stories the way we would share drugs on the street. That's what we gave one another: a boost out of Hill time to score stories.

· 3 ·

JESUS CHRIST WAS NORMAL

WHILE WE WERE PLAYING the Grudge Match for all it was worth back in the dorm, during the day I was getting assigned my Hill routine. You couldn't stay at the Diagnostic Center for more than three months. That's why they sent me to Belmont.

Since I came from a good home, they figured I had to be nuts to have done what I did. I went along with that because I didn't want to get stuck in Belmont. Plus, I thought maybe I was nuts. So when I was first called out of the cottage at the Diagnostic Center to talk to a psychologist, I remembered a story about a guy who was supposed to be nuts who told the shrink he had twelve souls, six were with Jesus Christ and six were with Machiavelli. When I tried this out on my shrink, she got excited and asked me about some book called *The Prince* that I'd never heard of. I figured it was written by Machiavelli. Then she asked me to finish the sentence "I saw. . . ." And I finished it with "the best minds of my generation dying." That got her even more excited, and she actually took a tranquilizer.

I knew she wanted stories gift wrapped. "One experience in Richard's childhood may shed some light on his distrust of others"—that sort of thing—good copy for a profile. So I gave her some—homemade, like little crafts made from Popsicle sticks. I told her that after my grandmother died, they made me kiss her in the coffin. (I never actually knew my grandmother well. I was sure she didn't like me, and I was nowhere near her funeral.) And I told the shrink I had a recurring dream about the incident. But I didn't give her any of the real stuff.

I passed the tests for the loony track, and I was only supposed to be on the Hill until they found a bin for me. When I went to the Belmont rehab lab, they gave me the whole line of tests, including seeing how fast I could put pegs in holes. After that, they pulled me out to talk to my counselor, Mr. Silver.

"Richard, how are you settling in?"

Sounded like a dumb question to me, so I shrugged my shoulders.

Then he asked, "What are you reading?"

I answered, "*Huckleberry Finn.*"

He smiled as though the title brought back memories. "What do you think of it?" he asked.

"I'd like to take a raft trip like that," I said.

"Yeah, so would I," he said.

"A couple of things bothered me, though," I told him. "When Huck is hiding out on Jackson's Island, people on a riverboat drop loaves of bread in the water with quicksilver in them, so they sink. The loaves float down the river and Huck picks them out and eats them!"

"So?"

"Have you ever been fishing and dropped a loaf of bread in the water?" I asked.

"I never have."

"You can't eat it, even after five seconds, let alone after it floats for an hour, let alone if it has sunk. Plus, when their raft gets rammed, Jim swims ashore and lights up a pipe. Where do the matches come from? In his hat! You ever tried to swim with a hat on? Let alone keep it so dry you could take a match from it and light it!"

Mr. Silver said, "Well, Richard, that'll be a good one for your thesis. I've been reading your file." He continued, "Frankly, they don't know what to do with you. You've tested very well indeed, and you don't cause trouble. However, in light of the crime you were sent here for, the judge is not likely to agree to allow you to return to the community. They think you may need some help. I'll be working with the psychologists to try to find a place that can give you that help. In the meantime, you're going to go to school in the mornings and work in the library in the afternoons."

Good, I thought. You just put me where I might not freak out until you find a bin for me. But mostly I was thinking about other things.

After waiting awhile for my reaction and not getting any, Mr. Silver said, "One piece of advice for you, Richard. You come from a good home and you're smart. That might make you want to look down on the other boys and keep your distance from them. Don't."

As usual, I thought he'd gotten his story all ass-backward. Most of the boys there came from poor families. Many of them had been abandoned by their parents or even mistreated. My family had always been good to me, but I didn't look down on any of the others. I just didn't trust them, and I didn't expect them to trust me.

I went to school starting the next morning. There were three teachers who took turns on different days and different shifts in the same room. It was a tough job, I guess. Some of the kids didn't know how to read and some did. They couldn't give homework since boys had jobs in the afternoon, and there was no place to do homework in the cottages. Nobody would do it if they assigned it anyway.

Mr. Waters was a college jock. I'm not sure what exactly he was supposed to be teaching. He didn't seem to have a clear idea of what he was supposed to do either. When the boys started getting rowdy, he would whine at them to get in line, which never worked.

Mr. Tyler was about as opposite Mr. Waters as you could get. He was a slight old guy who always wore a bow tie. He taught English, and everybody was always quiet during his class. Some kids would get really simple reading books like *See Spot Run.* He would sit with them in a circle and listen to them read and correct them. For the other kids, he'd give them grammar workbooks and come around now and then to check their work. He left me alone and let me read. He'd check on me now and then, talk to me about what I was reading, and suggest something else to read.

The third teacher, Mr. Anthony, came once a week to teach health. He was a tall black graduate student with tortoiseshell glasses, a mustache, and the style of clothes you might see on a man in a magazine. I imagined him having a James Bond life after school. I didn't know what he was studying, but I didn't think he was long for this work.

In Mr. Anthony's class we talked about sex. At first, some of the boys would start whooping and getting goofy around it, but Mr. Anthony would observe them as though they were some bug, and they'd cut it out. Out of class, boys started calling him the "Dick Doctor" or "Dick Doc." He taught us all about sexual development and about pregnancy and birth. He also wanted to know everything about how we talked about sex and what words we used.

We came from all different places in the state and had different ideas about sex and different words to express them. We argued about what we thought some of the words should mean. A big argument brewed about what a homosexual was. Some boys said you were queer only if you got corn-holed, not if you did it to another boy. They had a hard time when Mr. Anthony said, "Technically, a homosexual is anyone who engages in sexual acts with a partner of the same sex, regardless of their role in the sex act."

There was one issue that even Mr. Anthony didn't have the authority to settle. It was absolutely the all-time most provocative and controversial issue ever discussed on the Hill, namely, "Eating Pussy: Good or Bad?"

After lunch, I'd fall out and report for duty in the library. The librarian generally left me alone at first. She wore a cross necklace and spent her time straightening stuff, and when she wasn't doing that, she was reading. The library was part of the school building. I never once saw anybody visit the library, except for occasionally a kid sent by a teacher to pick up a particular book. Most of the time it was just Miss Lovitt and me, but we didn't talk too much, which was fine by me. She didn't care if I wandered off, so I started doing it regularly. She let me wander down to the end of the hall and out the side door. There was a stoop there where it was private and you could see fields and trees. I'd do yoga exercises from the book out there, or do push-ups, or dream.

It had been a mild spring. At the Diagnostic Center they had taken us out to play ball a lot. The fields now began to sear into July, and cicadas shook the summer air like maracas to a clave rhythm. I leaned back against the brick wall and looked toward the north over pastures that rolled to the bend of the James, with forests beyond to the horizon. I remembered searching for turtles in the woods near where I grew up. Each turn I took would be a new world; a shadow place of ferns and moss would turn into a bright tumble of rocks catching all the sunlight above the river.

It was in those woods that I first made out with a girl. We sat on a rock that was covered with emerald moss and phosphorescent teal lichens. Her name was Audrey. I was astonished that someone trusted me enough to prove it that way: wordless, soft, wet to me until my body rode up on a surge that washed all stories away. Audrey's mother lost custody and she had to move away to live with her dad.

I heard later that she got sent to the Barnet School for Girls.

When I first started at the library, Miss Lovitt asked me if I read any poetry. "Not much," I told her. The first book she turned me on to was by Robert Frost. I liked the way reading his poems was like visiting someplace I hadn't been to before. One day Miss Lovitt asked me what I was reading.

"You gave it to me, ma'am."

"No," she said. "I mean which poem?"

"Birches," I said.

"I know that poem. What do you think about it?"

"If it were me, I wouldn't care so much about swinging back to the ground."

Then she suggested a book by somebody named William Carlos Williams. I took it back to the cottage and read some poems on a weekend, but I couldn't make any sense of them. On Monday, I put the book back where it belonged on the shelf and didn't say anything. Miss Lovitt raised her head from her book and looked thoughtfully at where I'd put it back. Later she came by and asked me what I thought of it.

"I tried to read a couple of poems," I told her, "but I couldn't see them going anywhere."

"Can you give me an example?" Miss Lovitt asked.

"Do you know the poem about the red wheelbarrow?"

"Yes, I do," she said.

"How can so much depend on a wheelbarrow if he doesn't tell you what he wants to put in it and where he wants to wheel it? Especially if it's raining." She laughed.

Later she came back around with a list of books and said she wanted me to help her pick twenty of them to get for the library. I got to go over the whole thing and pick ones I knew and ask her about titles and authors I'd heard of but hadn't read.

Back in the cottage Mr. Lindquist noticed me putting books in my locker. Lining up for dinner one evening he walked over and said, "You like to read deep books? Really thought-provoking books?"

"I guess so," I said.

"The Bible," he said.

"What?"

"The Bible, the greatest scholars have studied over it for centuries, and they still don't understand it all."

Not likely, I thought. I was raised on Christianity, although I didn't know much of the Bible except secondhand. I don't guess I ever stopped believing in Jesus. I was about thirteen when I decided he was not on my side. I had gotten into one of a million arguments with my mom, and I made the mistake of trying to paraphrase scripture to her. "Jesus Christ said he came with a sword, to change people," I said.

And she said, "Jesus Christ was normal."

I didn't know it at the time, but that was the

beginning of when I stopped trusting Jesus. Around that time I had a bunch of dreams about my mother dying. Maybe what was really dying in those dreams was my trust in Jesus to be on my side. After that, it made sense to me that Jesus was the god of normal people. Schools were for normal people; courts and churches were for normal people. And there at the top of the normal pyramid was Jesus. Snickle had given me a new word for my story, out of his story about Shorty Nub. Maybe I was an "abomination in the eyes of the Lord." Wouldn't the shrinks love to get that story? My telling it to them was about as likely as my picking up the Bible.

To tell you the truth, there were times as I settled into the routine when I thought life on the Hill wasn't all bad. The Grudge Match was pretty amusing, and I was having some good times goofing with the boys. I felt healthy and clear from going to sleep at exactly the same time and getting up at the same time and eating the same amount of good food at the same times every day. Then there were books: I picked some up off the shelves, some of them Mr. Tyler turned me on to, and Miss Lovitt was throwing poems my way. I never knew where they would take me. Still, nothing seemed quite real, and time kept pressing heavier until I felt it would crush me.

· 4 ·

HOPPERGRASS

I'VE NEVER KNOWN anyone easier to be quiet with than
Miss Lovitt. Her presence did not require conversation. It expressed silence as she spoke and stillness as
she worked.

We had an intern in the library for a while named
Doug, a college student. He was way too skinny and
wore the same style clothes every day: madras shirt,
corduroys, and dirty buck shoes. The only thing that
changed was the color of his corduroys. Some days
they were gray and some days they were tan. His
hair was always trimmed perfectly to the middle of
his ears, and he wore black-framed glasses. Something about his teeth made him always hold his
mouth open a little bit, as though he were about to
drool. Because of that and his gangliness and his
habit of rolling his head and looking sideways when

he talked, it was hard for him to look serious no matter how hard he tried, and he tried hard.

He was always hyped up about a newspaper
article and always tried to get Miss Lovitt to agree
with him or to argue with him about it. Miss Lovitt
never did either. Doug read an article about welfare
and had to know where Miss Lovitt stood. "If the
Democrats had their way, we'd be giving a Cadillac
and twenty thousand dollars to every no-account
welfare slut for doing nothing but bringing another
illegitimate baby into the world."

Miss Lovitt was straightening the books. "Well,
even if they did," she said, "I'd still be concerned
about the mother and the child."

That got him cranked up even more, as though
he needed to talk louder for her to hear the point.
"But where do they think the money's going to
come from? How long do they think good family
people are going to work if they aren't allowed to
enjoy the fruits of their labor?"

It was as though she were talking to herself. "Yes,
I guess it always takes a lot to raise a family." Then,
switching to talk to him directly, "Doug, be a prince.
Open that mail and sort it."

You could tell that the rightness of his argument
stayed in him until he felt that he would bust with it.
He never tried to talk to me about the articles, but
he always seemed to think it would make him feel

better if he could give me orders, the way burping or farting relieves gas. If he couldn't get the Democrats or the welfare mothers to act right, and couldn't get Miss Lovitt to argue with him, he should at least be able to tell me what to do.

He was peeved. "Bowser, bring me a folder." I would have snapped to if Miss Lovitt had asked me, but he wasn't Miss Lovitt. Besides, I was into a book Mr. Tyler turned me on to, *The Grapes of Wrath*, and I must admit, I was thinking of me as an oppressed worker and him as a bad crew boss.

"I'm busy. Get it yourself."

Doug struggled for composure. "You don't look busy to me."

"I can't help that, Doug."

Miss Lovitt tuned out our squabbles, unless they got out of hand. "Boys, I'm going to the office. If anyone calls, I'll be back in a few minutes."

As soon as Miss Lovitt left us alone, Doug thought he could speak frankly. "You know, Bowser, when Miss Lovitt is gone, I'm your supervisor." He said "Bowser" loud and deep and drew it out, as though it was supposed to be an insult.

I was still trying to read. "I beg to differ with you, Junior."

I'd seen Doug's full name on a note that came over from the office: Douglas Washington Branch Jr. Calling him "Junior" always worked.

Doug's face was flushing. "That's the way it is. Ask Miss Lovitt, and she'll tell you."

I said, "I most humbly must beg to differ with you, Junior."

Doug was breathing deeply. "You can beg all day if you want, Bowser, but if you piss me off, you're going down." He really liked saying, "You're going down." Maybe he got it from *Dragnet*.

"Kiss my ass, Junior," I said. Doug made a big point of keeping his cool. He came up next to me where I was reading and sat on the table with his feet on the chair. He was gawking down at me through his black-framed glasses with his mouth open a little and his hands clasped around the edge of the table, like a judge.

"Bowser," he said, drawing it out again and trying to make it sound silly. "That sounds like a dog's name. How'd you get called that?"

"My mother's a bitch." I was still hoping he'd go away.

"Real funny, Bowser. What did you do to get sent here?"

"Nothing. I was a victim of circumstance," I said.

"Oh, yeah, nothing's ever your fault, is it?"

"Never," I said. "I blame society."

"Well, you're doing okay here, aren't you? Other people are feeding you and you don't have to lift a finger."

I had given up on reading. I had closed the book and was staring at him the way you stare at a punk. "Yeah, I was going to check into the Holiday Inn, but I heard you have better room service. As a matter of fact, I could use a drink right now. Why don't you run and fetch me something, Junior."

Just then, Miss Lovitt came back and said to Doug, "Please don't put your feet on the chair."

"Where the hell were you raised, Junior, in a barn?" I added.

Miss Lovitt said, "Cut it out, Bowser."

Doug tried to look at me with contempt, but he looked like he had gas. I went back to my book, and Doug started reading the newspaper. After a few minutes he started chuckling to himself and shaking his head. He couldn't hold it in and started again with Miss Lovitt. "Those Democrats!" If I had to hear any more Doug talk, I was afraid I would do harm to myself or others.

"Miss Lovitt," I said, "I'm going to go check on things at the stoop." Miss Lovitt nodded to me with a pained expression, like she wished she could go too.

Out in the hall, I spotted someone between me and the door with a broom in his hand. It was a bright day and the door was open, so I could see the rays streaming in and making a Milky Way of dust around him, but I couldn't make out his face. I was within fifteen feet of him before I recognized it was

Nose. It was too late to go in another direction. Besides, I'd rather get my ass kicked than have to listen to Doug.

I didn't want to, but I walked straight toward him. He stopped sweeping. I couldn't see the expression on his face. "Professor," he said, leaning on his broom, and I could see a big smile, even with the light coming from behind his head. "Come here and look at something." He leaned the broom against the wall and led me into a boiler room. "Have a seat," he said. I sat down on an old school chair. "Coffee?" he asked, like this was a business meeting or something. Sure enough, there was a card table in the boiler room, and it had a jar of instant coffee on it with some creamer and a little bowl of sugar.

He gave me a Styrofoam cup with some instant coffee in it and poured hot water on it from a thermos. "I want to show you something," he said. I was getting nervous and started tearing at the rim of the cup until he came back from behind the boiler with a covered jar. When he saw that I had been chipping at his cup, he held the jar back, looked at me sternly, and said, "You ain't got to be tearing up my cup." He was thoughtful as he sat down with the jar. Then, leaning forward, he held the jar out to me. I was wondering if it had drugs in it, or something he stole, or a body part. There was grass on the bottom and a stick leaning against the side. Then there was a sudden movement in the jar, and I could see it was alive. Nose smiled big. "Hoppergrass," he said in triumph. "I like a hoppergrass."

We looked at the insect for a while until Nose broke the silence. "Shoot me a fog, man." I pulled out a Camel for him and one for me. We smoked them down to the butts, then carefully put out the butts and put them in our pockets for later. "I usually won't smoke a duck after a white boy. Most of them eat pussy." He contemplated the jar again. "You don't eat no pussy. You got my back with Mr. Lindquist," Nose said. "I can't control myself sometime when I'm mad. If I done smacked Mr. Lindquist, they'd've beat the hell out of me. If they even had me for scrapping, they'd be shooting me a six for sure."

"It's okay," I said. "I don't expect to be here for my first progress." Nose looked in the jar and waited for me to explain. "They think I'm crazy. They're trying to send me to a hospital."

Nose thought about it and asked, "They got girls there?"

I said, "I bet they do."

He repeated after me, laughing and shaking his head, "I bet they do."

He jiggled the jar and watched the hoppergrass jump. "Professor, where you from anyway?"

I said, "Richmond. How about you?"

"Petersburg. You ever been to Petersburg?" he asked.

"No," I said. "You ever been to Richmond?"

Nose said, "No. You ever been to Washington, DC?"

"Sure," I said, "lots of times."

His eyes got really bright, and he smiled and said, "Damn. I been there, too. You my homeboy, Professor! And I tell you what. You give me a go with them dukes. What you want to do when you get out, Professor?"

"I don't know," I said. "What do you want to do?"

Me, when I get out of here, I want to be a store man. Before Mumma took us to Petersburg, she was raising four of us in Stevensville: me and my two brothers and my sister. My uncle had a little store called D&P Market, because he was Fred Davis and the other man was named Parker.

When I was little, it looked to me like people got they money from the government office or from selling a hog or something and then they all give it to the store man. When the paper ships was loading at West Point, all the men'd be hanging around the D&P Market at evening time and standing in line to cash their checks and buy wine. It look to me like they was making beaucoup

48

money, Jack, and it look like all the money in the world go straight to Uncle Fred's hand.

And Uncle Fred give us some cans of food or some seed or feed, even if we didn't have no money. He write it all in a big book and let it slide until Mumma get her check. And he do that for everybody and kept on doing it too, even though sometime he never see that money. And I was just a little boy, looking at Uncle Fred there, looking down at that book over his glasses and writing with a pencil, and I say, "That's what I want. I'm going to be a store man my own self. And if somebody needs something but ain't got money, I just going to front it to them and write it real careful with a sharp pencil in my own big book."

I offered him another Camel. "I want to get a motorcycle and travel around the country," I said.

"Where do you want to go?" Nose asked.

"New York, Vermont, Oklahoma, California, down the Mississippi—everywhere. I want to go to different towns and meet people. When I get bored, I'll get back on my bike and move on. Then I'll go back now and then to see my friends in all the places I've been. If they're in any kind of trouble, I'll help them out. If the bank has taken their land or somebody's cheated them or bullied them, I'll call my friends from other

49

towns, and they'll come as soon as they hear from me. I'll call on the phone and say, 'The skillet is hot,' and they will get on their bikes without asking any questions and come to wherever I am. Then there'll be a gang of us and we'll straighten things out."

Nose was tilting back smoking as I talked, and I could tell that he could picture what I was saying just fine.

The next day I was hanging out on the stoop and decided to look and see if Nose was in the boiler room. He wasn't there, so I turned on the light and thought I'd look around a little. There were some shelves for storage in the corner and I walked over and started poking around. There were screws and fasteners, duct tape, old shingles, parts to lawn chairs, and some things I didn't even recognize. I noticed a box that said CLEANING SUPPLIES on it and opened it up: Windex, Pine-Sol, Bon Ami, and a little bottle of spot remover with the brand name Carbona on it. I took out the little bottle of Carbona and put the box back on the shelf. Afterward, I slipped the little bottle under my belt beneath the shirt and kept it out of sight until I could stow it in a cookie package in my locker before supper.

Back in the cottage after supper Evan took me aside to listen to his radio under the stairs. We'd already been doing that for a while, and Mr. Lindquist didn't say anything about it. This time Evan brought his little Eiffel Tower picture book with him. He showed me a picture of his older sister in a white lace dress posed at a piano with sad blue eyes facing the camera and long black hair flowing down her pale neck.

"She's a knockout," I said.

"Don't say any more about her," he said. He'd snuck the book out and was showing it to me like this was very special and he didn't want anyone to know he had it. Maybe he was even afraid that I might say something crude.

"No," I said, "I just mean she's pretty and looks like she must be smart and nice."

"Smart? She's on the honor roll every marking period. See this picture? That was after she won first prize in a piano competition."

We stopped talking and listened to "Lay Lady Lay," on the radio. When a commercial came on, I asked, "What do you want to do when you get out of here, Evan?"

"I don't know," he replied. "I'm getting good at the barbershop. Maybe I could go home for a while and get a job cutting hair. I could move out of the house and invite Connie to move in with me. Constance is her full name, and it fits her. She never says a bad word about anybody, no matter how mean they are to her. She's been lame from birth, and it seems like everybody but me gives her a hard time.

The kids won't even say hello to her because she limps. Mom's always telling her she has to work twice as hard and be twice as good as anyone else, because she can't count on finding a man who'll look after her. I guess Mom figures she has the right. My dad left her alone to take care of us when I was a baby."

· 5 ·

NOTHING BUT TIME

NEXT AFTERNOON, I dropped by the boiler room again, and this time Nose was sitting under the light playing solitaire. "Have a seat," he said.

"What do you do here, Nose?" I asked him.

"You mean for work?" Nose answered. "I work for Mr. Woodrow. If a gutter busts or a light needs changing, we fix it. Sometimes I clean up over here at the school too, but half the time I just hang out here in my office."

I heard the door creak behind me and turned to see a big black man. I was a little scared, but the big man looked gentle all over. Even the way he stood was gentle. His face was broad with lines weathered into the skin all around his eyes, as though they were made by smiling outside in the sun.

The man seemed to find the sight of me amusing,

and he staggered back in mock surprise. "Well, pardon me, gentlemen. I did not know y'all was having a convention."

Nose grinned at him. "This here is my homeboy."

The big man looked curious. "Homeboy got a name?"

"Yes, sir," I said. "They call me Bowser."

Nose introduced the big man to me. "This here is my boss, Mr. Woodrow. He's head of maint'ance."

Mr. Woodrow continued to act formal and seemed to be having a good time. "And may I ask why a white boy is called by the name of a dog?"

"Well, sir, my real name is Richard Grover. When I showed up at the Diagnostic Center, one boy thought he heard me called Rover. We had nothing much to do, so they kept joking and laughing about it until, by lunchtime, they had decided if I was going to have a dog's name, they may as well call me Bowser."

"I'll tell you what," Nose added, "Bowser'll give you a go with the dukes!"

"And may I ask where Mr. Bowser dog work?"

"The library, sir," I answered.

Mr. Woodrow nodded thoughtfully. "They got funny books in that lib'ary?"

I was starting to smile. "No, sir."

Mr. Woodrow seemed taken aback. "No funny books! Now I ask you, Mr. Bowser dog, what the hell good is a lib'ary like that?"

I could just manage to answer without laughing, "I can't say, sir."

"You can't say! You can't say! Well, ain't you done your *reconnoitering*?" When Mr. Woodrow and Nose saw me red-faced and confused about how to answer that one, all three of us broke down howling and laughing.

"Bowser dog, I bet you know how to have a good time." Woodrow made it sound like the biggest compliment in the world and I took it that way.

Nose was looking at the hoppergrass in the jar. Mr. Woodrow had straddled a chair with a cup of coffee in his hand and watched him. "Let me see that jar, Nose. When you going to let him out?"

"I don't keep them more than a day."

"Has he been up for progress yet?" I joked.

Nose smiled. "No progress for my hoppergrass. I just bring him in for a visit and then send him on his way."

Mr. Woodrow chuckled.

You love them hoppergrass, don't you, Nose? But I tell you there ain't no future in them. If you going to be bringing something in from out o' doors, you ought to think about watermelons. When I was your age, there was a man named Dr. Bathhurst who lived down the road, and he kept the nicest watermelon patch I ever seen. As soon as they was good and ripe, we used to crawl on our bellies under his fence and make off with the biggest ones we could carry. One early morning we go to that patch and see a sign there that say ONE OF THESE WATERMELONS IS POISONED. So my brother Jack say, "Y'all wait here a minute." And he come back after a while with a pail of paint and a brush. He crawled into that patch and go up to that sign and crossed out the ONE and write TWO on top of it so it say, TWO OF THESE WATERMELONS IS POISONED. We never got no more water-melons from Dr. Bathhurst, but people tell the story of how Jack outsmarted the Doc ever since.

———

When I went back to the cottage, I kept thinking of my time with Nose and Mr. Woodrow and replayed Mr. Woodrow's story. Some of the lines cracked me up just remembering them. I was in a good mood right through supper. Evan and I swapped stories in the evening, and that was nice too.

The next day was Saturday, and Mr. Lindquist took the cottage out to play baseball. I liked the game, but I wasn't any good. When I was in the field, I always thought the ball was coming down in front of me when it was coming down behind or the other way around. If nothing happened for a while I would start to dream. When I was up, I held the bat with my elbow angled so that it looked like I would slam the ball a mile. The first few games the boys on the other team would yell, "Move back!" when I came to the plate, but after a while they started to notice that I never, ever hit the ball.

That morning while we were still at the round table in the cottage, I said, "I think I'll sit out the game and read today." Snicklesnort said, "Yeah, why don't you sit out, like, every day." And from that day on, I did. I found a big, spreading oak up the hill from the diamond, and I'd take a couple books there. Sometimes I read. Sometimes I just dreamed. A lot of times, though, another boy would choose not to play and would come by the tree to talk.

The others started to call the tree "the professor's office." I had two names now on top of my real name, which nobody ever used other than adults. When they called me Bowser, I was just another kid, as in "Bowser can't play ball worth a shit," or "Bowser'll give you a go with the dukes." They called me Professor if they wanted me on their side of an argument, as in "Professor say there ain't no governor of the world," or when they were asking me a question, as in "Hey, Professor, how do you spell an F?" They also called me Professor when they were talking about the office I held under the tree on Saturday, as in "I ain't playing today. I'm going to the professor's office."

Even black boys would come to my office, and

nobody said anything. Miles came up one day to get some help writing a letter. Miles didn't talk much, but the other black boys would stop talking whenever he spoke, even if he didn't raise his voice. He always looked like he was watching everything that was going on around him, and like he was concerned and didn't approve.

Miles was stumped on a letter to a girl at the Barnet School for Girls. This one started, *Time: Doomsday. Place: Behind Prison Walls. Song: I want you, I need you, I love you.*

"That's a good start," I said.

Miles said he'd gotten the lines from Nose.

"So what may I help you with, Miles?" I asked.

Miles said, "Professor, I could get next to this girl, you know? Like a Temptations song or something." I pulled out my yellow legal pad and wrote on it, *You are the torch in the dark cavern of my soul*, and I handed it to him.

He bent over it for a moment, then looked up and smiled.

"You are a poet, Professor." Then he leaned back with a piece of grass in his mouth and watched the ballplayers. After a while he said, "You know, I usually won't smoke a duck after a white boy."

Nose never came by my office, which I was glad about. He was a good ballplayer. Besides, we both knew it wouldn't do either of us good for people to know about us being homeboys at work.

All through July it was so bright we had to cover our eyes with our hands when we were outside just to see anything. Not a drop of rain had fallen since I came to the Hill, and the fields were brown. Nose and I would hang out together in the shade on the stoop or in the boiler room almost every day. Neither one of us had that much work to do, and neither of our bosses minded. Sometimes Mr. Woodrow would come by just to swap stories.

On one of those bright afternoons, Nose had come out to look for a hoppergrass, and we ended up lying on our backs with our heads on our folded arms, inspecting the drifting clouds. Mr. Woodrow came by and sat down for a break. He pulled some Red Man out of the hip pocket of his overalls and started to chew. The stoop was on the northeast end of the building, so it was shady in the afternoon.

"Hey, Nose," I asked, "how'd you get sent here anyway?" The question had entered my mind like a cloud drifting into view in the sky.

"That's a long story, Professor. I don't know if you got the time for it."

"I got nothing but time," I said.

"You ain't doing nothing but time either," Nose said. All three of us savored that one for a minute.

Then Mr. Woodrow said, "Go ahead, Nose. I don't believe I know that whole story my own self."

—————

It was last August and hotter than it is now. Me and Simple, and Eddy and Pork George and Roberto, was hanging every day, just to think up something with juice to do. A couple days we rode a bus out to Hopewell to clean and oil the brass plates on the graves in the Jewish graveyard they call a memorial park. But that only paid a buck ten a hour, and they left us out on the graves after we oiled them all. We played games, like to see which one died the oldest and which grave was the oldest, but it get too hot for that.

Down on Jackson Street there was a place where they'd knocked down the Jackson Villa Apartments after they all crumbled. There was still a brick wall there between the vacant lot and the street. We just called it the wall, and that's where we knew to find each other. Five of us was there every day sooner or later. There be kids coming over from other streets too sometime, and we got a gang as big as twenty some nights before the cops come and break us up.

One morning Pork George come by with some hot dogs he lifted from the Winn-Dixie. We made a fire behind some rubble next to the wall in the vacant lot and roasted them. While they was cooking, Simple say, "Hey, what if you was to cook these here hot dogs over a fire with pot in it, you think you'd get high when you ate them?"

Nobody knew what to say. Then Eddy say real loud, "Hey!" like he figured out the answer. "Hey, Simple. I got a question for you. Why do they call you Simple?" Everybody cracked up laughing.

And about every five minutes after that, somebody say, "Hey, Simple. Why do they call you Simple?" And we all cracked up again.

That was only going to keep us going for but so long. We all tried to think of what to do next.

We started to get real bored when Roberto asked, "You think we could get any more work at the Jewish graveyard?"

Eddy say, "I damn sure ain't polishing no more grave plates." Nobody argued with him, but I see that graveyard in my head, with a big old pond in the middle of it filled with white ducks.

I say, "Listen here. Why don't we go out to duck hunt today?"

Pork George go, "What the hell you talking about?"

I sort of come up with the plan at the same time as telling it.

Everybody split up to find other kids to join, and then go home to lift any flashlights and pillowcases and bread and crackers they could find. We was all to meet back up at the wall before five o'clock.

I waited in the vacant lot to watch everybody come

61

over the wall in twos and threes toting pillowcases. Simple brought his little brother, Smiley. Pork George picked up a bunch of kids I never seen before. Smiley was only ten, and a couple of boys was older than me.

When we get on the bus, I paid for all eighteen of us together. This fat old driver say, "What you boys up to with them pillowcases?"

And I say, "We minding our own business. Long as I pay everybody's fare, why don't you mind your business too?"

"I tell you what," he say. "You bother any of my passengers, your business and your ass both be mine."

There was only three other folks on the bus. There was a white boy about my age with a girl. He had long hippie hair, and she had a flowered dress on. They both looked out the window real hard and peeked at us out the corner of their eyes until they got off at the next stop. Then there was an old black preacher with gray hair and a Bible in his lap who sat right behind the driver. I tried to keep all the boys straight, but you know how so many boys together want to get gang tough and cause trouble.

The little boys was yelling and bouncing all around, and you couldn't make them mind. The preacher had his nose stuck in the Bible like he didn't know we was there until Roberto start to razz at him.

He say, "Hey, old man." The preacher didn't pay him no mind. "*Old man with a BOOK!*"

The driver looked at us through his mirror and yelled,

"Don't make me have to stop this bus and come back there and throw you boys off by your britches."

The old preacher say, "These boys ain't bothering me." He put the Bible down on his seat and stood up in the aisle to face the back of the bus. He was much taller than I thought. He stood there not saying a word and looked a long time at the boy that yelled at him, like Roberto raised his hand to be called on and the preacher was waiting for him to answer. When Roberto didn't say nothing, the preacher kept standing there, with each hand on a seat back, and took his time to look around at us—look straight into a boy's eyes or not, just as he pleased. He made us all feel like he asked us a question, and he waiting for an answer that we didn't know.

The preacher opened his mouth to talk, and every one of us boys kept his mouth shut and didn't stir. "'And take heed to yourselves, lest at any time your hearts be overcharged with surfeiting, and drunkenness, and cares of this life, and so that day come upon you unawares. For as a snare shall it come on all them that dwell on the face of the whole earth. Watch ye therefore, and pray always, that ye may be accounted worthy to escape all these things that shall come to pass, and to stand before the Son of man.' THUS SAYETH THE LORD. AMEN."

When he sat back down, Pork George must've felt a little ashamed because he had to get a word in. "That grizzly old preacher act like he going to do something.

He ain't going to do shit." But he didn't put a lot of heart into it.

When we got off the bus, the sun was just starting to go down, and there wasn't a cloud in the sky. We started to walk along the train tracks toward the graveyard, everybody pumped and talking the plan, adding a little here and wanting to make a little change there, but mostly in the mood and having a good time. When we got to where you cross the road to get to the graveyard, we look across and see the sign with the star on it that say BETH SHALOM MEMORIAL GARDEN, and we looked up and down the street to see that they's no car coming, and sent boys across about four at a time.

Everybody knew what they's supposed to do. Two boys went in with pillowcases full of bread crumbs and started to spread them on the ground near the bank and move back with a flock of ducks after them. The younger boys headed off to the shore of the pond, between the shore and the ducks. All the rest of the boys creeped up in the bushes and then fanned out toward the pond so the ducks was in the middle. The little boys waited quiet as we opened our pillowcases. Then I hollered, "QUACK!"

The little boys turned they flashlights on the ducks and started to herd them to us yelling "QUACK QUACK QUACK QUACK QUACK." Since the lawn had just been watered, boys was slipping and sliding after them ducks and running into each other in the mud, and the ducks was flapping and quacking. I jumped for one of

64

them and fell flat but got him by the foot. Then I hopped on him and got my arms around his wings. Simple dived after a duck and hit me, and we was rolling around on top of each other in the mud with ducks quacking and flapping everywhere. By the end of it, we got about twenty ducks in pillowcases and met up back at the sign with the Jewish star on it.

———

Nose paused. I watched a cloud drift and asked, "So you got sent up for stealing ducks?

"Nah, but like I say, it's a long story."

"Well," said Mr. Woodrow, "you going to have to finish it another time. Time for us to go in."

As the summer wore on, I could have started settling into Hill time, but I wouldn't let myself. It was like the Jack London story where the man is freezing to death. He starts to feel warm and cozy, but he knows if he lets himself sleep he won't wake up. I kept myself awake with stories. Past stories from the street mixed up with stuff I was reading and the stories about my motorcycle and my big ride.

I tried to steer clear of some stories, but after a while my story time got wound too tight and would spin off anywhere. One evening in late July, I was lying back under the stairs with Evan. We had the radio playing low, and he was talking about how he was going to open a barbershop when he got out. Then he started telling me more stories about his life on the street and how worried he was about what would happen to Constance. Most of his stories were about saving Constance.

I knew what it was like to want to save someone. Bradley Davis was in my class in both fifth and sixth grades, but they didn't make him do any work. They just let him sit and doodle all day. Then in seventh grade they sent him to some special school during the day, but we hung out more than ever after school.

I don't know what was wrong with him. Someone may have thought he was retarded, but when I gave him books, we read them and talked about them. After reading *Tom Sawyer* and *Huckleberry Finn*, we even hung out in the woods and tried to build a raft. The only thing I could see unusual about him was that he had a facial tic, especially when he got nervous.

One day we were down in the woods and had walked all the way to a point of rocks over the river. Two older hardrocks I knew climbed up the path from the river and came upon us. They started teasing Bradley the way they do when they're picking a fight. Billy Mason started, "What's the matter with your face? Why does it keep twitching?" Bradley, of course, twitched more when he was scared, and he couldn't answer. "Don't you make them faces at me when I'm talking to you!"

I had always been okay with Billy; he knew I got in trouble a lot, so we had something in common. I took him aside and said, "He can't help it, man; he's retarded." The other, older boy was listening too. They laughed and patted me on the back, then went over and apologized to Bradley and went on their way. We were both quiet most of the way up the path toward home.

Bradley asked, "What did you say to Billy Mason?"

I said, "That you're a good guy." I know he didn't believe me. Ever since, I have been sure he actually heard what I said to Billy.

In the middle of seventh grade, Bradley came out one morning to help me with my paper route. He was upset, and I asked him what was wrong. Bradley's father was a brutal man who beat his mother. That morning, Bradley said his father had signed papers for him to be sent to a place called Fishersville.

"Where's that?" I asked.

"I don't know," he said. "They say I can come home some weekends, but I don't think Dad would drive that much to pick me up. Dad kept telling me it's the best thing for me, and it would be like a camp, and I could learn to do a job and make money. But Mom kept crying until Dad hit her, and she went out somewhere."

My dad got home late most nights. I waited up for him that night, lying in bed and thinking about how he always knew what to do. Maybe he would suggest that we adopt Bradley and let him move in with us.

I heard the downstairs door open, and I slipped out of bed and ran down to greet Dad.

"What are you doing out of bed so late?" He took off his hat and coat and gave me a big hug, but he was tired.

"I waited up for you, Dad, because I need your help."

"Did you get in trouble in school today?" he asked wearily.

"No, it's not me, Dad. It's for Bradley."

"Bradley?"

"Yeah, Dad. They're going to send him away."

Dad got himself a drink, then came back in the living room and sat in the big easy chair facing me. "Son, I'm sure Bradley's parents are doing what's best for him."

"No, Dad. Bradley's father beats his mother. They might just be trying to get rid of him."

Then Dad slowed and focused the way he does when he is explaining something important that he thinks I might not understand. "Son, you know yourself that Bradley is not quite right. He needs special help, and we are not in a position to know what help is best for him. You know, a boy like that can seem all right sometimes, and then they can change and behave differently. As he gets older, I know we'll all feel better if he gets the help he needs."

I felt ashamed of Bradley getting sent away. Maybe it was because I couldn't do anything about it. Maybe it was because I thought I was like him in some ways. I didn't do well in school either; I often fell to dreaming and wouldn't listen or do my work. I never stopped looking up to my dad, and I never stopped knowing that he loved me, but I never stopped wondering if he didn't think I "wasn't quite right" myself.

My mom worshipped Dad. He was normal, the way Jesus was. And she lived to be normal enough for him. She devoted herself to the Church, and she wanted her worship and her home to be just right— fashionable but not overboard. And she said little prayers out loud to "normal" all the time: "Well, well, it will be all right," "One day at a time," and "Tomorrow is another day."

Mom was from a good family in New England, and she had gone to school in interior design for one year. She had no natural Southern accent, but she cultivated one that sounded like an accent that no one else in the world had but her.

I don't know what happened to her to make her

afraid or even what she was afraid of. Whatever it was, she thought the only thing that could protect her was being normal.

Meanwhile on our TV, I watched protesters getting beaten and chased by dogs in Alabama and people being killed in Vietnam: soldiers, civilians, women, and children. Matters in general made less and less sense. Both Mom and Dad love me. I know that. They stood by me even with all the disgrace I brought to them and their good name and their normalcy.

When Bradley Davis came back from Fishersville, he was sixteen. He didn't go back to school. He got a job as the custodian at an apartment building instead and bought himself an old Buick convertible. We became friends again and took all kinds of dope together until he got killed and I got sent up.

Some stories I can't stand, like the story of Bradley Davis. Once I let a bad story in, more start coming in a river.

· 6 ·

SPOTS IN MY NOSE

Sunday morning after chapel some white adults came out on a bus to lead us in activities. They took us out behind the cottage and were leading a game where they spread out a parachute and put a dodgeball on it, and you try to bounce off the other side's half of the parachute. Nose was playing hard and rallying his team, and that made it more lively for everyone.

I didn't choose to play. I was lying back with Snicklesnort and Evan and Babybird under a tree. It seemed like a lazy day, but I was wound really tight. My story time got moving too fast, and it seemed more real than Hill time. It was out there spinning faster and faster, with nothing holding it down.

"I got something for you," I said, and pulled the little bottle of Carbona out from under my shirt. As the three boys watched, I removed my sock and soaked it with the spot remover. Then I lay back, put the sock over my nose and mouth, and huffed. Everything hummed, like a sound that was coming forward, drawing back, coming forward, going big, getting small—in a fog, echoing sounds and colors too. I felt sick to my stomach.

I was just about to pass the rag to Snicklesnort when I felt a bang on the left side of my head. I couldn't see or think straight. It took me a minute to realize that Nose had slugged me full on my face— and was looming over me.

"Get up, you son of a bitch. What the hell you think you doing? You got no business hanging out with these pussy-eating motherfuckers."

Snickle and Evan hadn't yet huffed anything. They both jumped on Nose. Snickle shot his cuff, so he went down. Evan was on top of him, holding him with his left hand and punching him in the face with his right. I sat against the tree watching, with the sounds and the colors fading, jumping forward, tumbling back in a sickening pulse.

Gray waded into the fight, seeming to get bigger as he squared off. He came up behind Evan and slugged him on the side of the face so hard that Evan rolled over, bleeding. Babybird jumped on Gray from behind, but Gray flipped him like a sack of flour. Miles was going at Snicklesnort, throwing punches and jumping way back like a kangaroo.

Mr. Lindquist screamed, "You want to fight some-body, you fight me," but nobody was listening. He ran into the cottage to call for help, and in a minute, a car pulled up with Mr. Ball and Shorty Nub. Shorty Nub was holding a short wooden bat in his hand.

At first, Mr. Lindquist was saying things like "You going to fight somebody, fight me" and "All right, boys, that's enough" while trying to pull guys off by their shoulders. When Gray knocked Evan off him, Nose rolled over on top of Evan and started pum-meling Evan's face in a rage. Mr. Ball could see that Evan was going to get hurt bad, so he grabbed Nose by his shoulders, pulled him off, and bellowed at him, "Hands on your head!"

Nose stood up and seemed to get hold of himself. He put his hands on his head, but Shorty Nub walked up behind Nose and kicked him straight in the ass. Nose lost it. He turned and lunged at the Nub, but Shorty Nub slammed him in the head with his bat—a full swing from the shoulder with all his weight behind it. Nose went down to his knees right there at my feet, bleeding, and passed out. The Nub looked like he might haul off and kick him where he lay.

Mr. Ball saw the whole thing, and he smiled. Mr. Lindquist turned from trying to get Miles and Snickle apart in time to see Nose go down. He ran up behind Shorty Nub and put him in a full nelson. Shorty Nub was struggling and cussing. Mr. Ball was as relaxed as ever and seemed to be enjoying himself. He hollered out, "Put your hands on your heads *NOW!*" We all did.

Mr. Lindquist kept saying to Shorty Nub, "The boy's down; he could be hurt." That didn't seem to calm Shorty Nub. Then Mr. Lindquist said, "You might have killed him," which got Shorty Nub's attention.

"That black bastard tried to kill me," Shorty Nub said, pulling his arm away from Mr. Lindquist.

Mr. Ball was kneeling over Nose and looking at the wound on his head. "Yeah, this boy would surely have done you harm. I saw it all up close, Mr. Palmer. [That was Shorty Nub's name to adults.] You did what you had to. I'm going in to call an ambulance."

Nose was taken off to the hospital, which was good. On the Hill, if you do either of two things, they have to beat the hell out of you: if you try to run or if you fight an adult. And they'll beat you half to death. Everybody knew that was Shorty Nub's specialty. They took Evan off to the infirmary. His left cheek was like a cantaloupe where Gray had slugged him, and his nose was a bloody mess from Nose punching him.

Mr. Lindquist was pissed. He told the activity leaders to go on with the parachute and dodgeball game, and he called out everyone he'd seen fighting:

Snicklesnort, Babybird, Gray, Miles, me. He marched us all into the cottage basement, and he made us sit around the closest round table in front of his desk. "What the hell were you boys thinking? You know Mr. Palmer would have taken you all up to the admin building if I hadn't stopped him?" They took you to a room in the admin building to beat you if you ran or fought a staff person. We all knew that Nose was likely to be the only one taken up there, since nobody else went at an adult.

Babybird was all cranked up and started spilling. "Nose jumped on Bowser and hit him, Mr. Lindquist. We weren't doing nothing but trying to protect him." The sights and sounds going in and out were getting a little calmer now, but my head was pounding and foggy and my stomach didn't feel good. I knew there was something I should be saying, but I just wanted to lie down.

Babybird kept warming to his story; it made him a hero defending me against the black boys. "Mr. Lindquist, you know Nose has been after Bowser ever since he got here. He started that fight in the shower, and he's been pissed off ever since Bowser wore his underpants. Everybody knows Nose has just been waiting for the right time to go at Bowser and he'll kill him if he can. He saw his chance when you all were taking a break, and he just walked over to Bowser and laid into him. I bet Nose told Gray and Miles to wait until Nose threw the first punch and then jump in. It was a setup, Mr. Lindquist."

Gray and Miles were slouching low in their seats, not even bothering to look at Mr. Lindquist—arms folded, hardrocks. Miles said in his slow, deep voice that sounded almost bored, "Yeah, we jumped in, all right. We jumped in when we saw you four pussy white boys punching out on one Nose." Gray and Miles were talking to Snicklesnort, who was staring off into space, not to Mr. Lindquist. They could stand for whatever the man would throw at them, and they damn sure weren't going to seek drag.

"Bowser?" Mr. Lindquist looked at me. I just felt sick and shook my head. Mr. Lindquist probably thought I was being stand-up in some way—refusing to rat on another boy, even if it was Nose. He got that steely-eyed marine look and said, "You all are going on special force starting tomorrow, and there's nothing I can do about it."

The next morning during lineup after breakfast, I started to fall out when they called for special force, but Mr. Lindquist walked up behind me and grabbed me by the arm. "Not you," he said. So I went to school in the morning, and in the afternoon I went to the library.

I looked for Nose in his office, even though I knew he wouldn't be there. I found his hoppergrass and looked at him in the jar for a while. It was funny how that little insect could absorb your attention. I watched him and played with him for a few minutes. Then I took him out to the stoop, let him go, and watched him hop away.

At dinner that evening, I sat next to Ben Susan. Ben Susan's job was actually in the cottage helping Mrs. Lindquist, washing windows and whatnot. To the adults he seemed small and harmless. They would have never given him the job if they saw him the way we did. Anyway, Mrs. Lindquist loved to talk, and Ben Susan got the scoop from her on all kinds of business.

Ben Susan figured I would want the news on my locker mate. "Evan has only a broken nose and bruises. They keep him in the infirmary tonight; they put him on force tomorrow."

"What about Nose?" I asked.

"They say Nose have broke his head. He is in the infirmary now."

"Did they say it was a concussion?"

Ben Susan was straining to remember the exact words but couldn't.

"Are they going to put him on special force?" I asked.

"They going to keep him in the infirmary until his head's okay. Then they put him on special force. I don't know how you can get at him."

I didn't know what he was talking about at first, and then I realized that he thought what everyone would think. Evan got hurt defending me from Nose. They were going to be watching for me to take Nose out using whatever I had to. Ben Susan looked around the dining hall. He nudged me with his elbow to look under the table where he was holding a steel wire wrapped around two bent spoons. I took it from him and put it into my pocket. I don't know why. Maybe I just didn't know how to explain everything to Ben Susan. I also had a feeling that his gift could come in handy somehow.

Back in the cottage, I pulled out the wire and put it in my locker so no one else could see. It was a homemade garrote. Ben Susan had taken some wire Mrs. Lindquist might have used to hang pictures, and he made two handles out of spoons he stole from Mrs. Lindquist's kitchen. I figured I'd hide it in the locker until morning and then carry it with me during the day. After the fight they were probably checking lockers, but they always did it while we were away at school or work. If I needed to, I could stow it in a hiding place under a brick by the stoop near the library. Snicklesnort had it together enough to pick up the Carbona after the fight and stashed it later in the bottom of the cottage trash bag, so I thought I was okay there.

I was heading for my table when Mr. Lindquist

called me. "Bowser, come here." He beckoned me into the passageway going toward the showers, the only private place to talk. "Why the hell would any fool want to put a rag full of spot remover over his face?" His face was red, but he seemed genuinely mystified. "To get high?"

I figured someone had told him the truth. "No, sir. I'll be honest with you. I got spots in my nose."

Mr. Lindquist was furious. "You think that's funny, boy? I have seen fine men die because some asshole was funny like that." I had to hold my head down, so he couldn't see my face. I was trying to remember what movie had that line in it. I was pretty sure Mr. Lindquist was acting a part in a movie, but I couldn't remember which one, and it was cracking me up.

"Bowser, you asshole, you get people to want to help you. Then you fuck yourself up and fuck them up with you. You got those shrinks thinking you're crazy, but you're not. You're just an asshole." Mr. Lindquist walked off disgusted. I knew he was right. That was exactly it, and he said it just right and I was disgusted too. I was trying not to think about Nose in the hospital and my table boys on special force and nothing happening to me. Worst, this would mean Nose had no chance of pulling a three next progress.

It seemed none of the boys was blaming it on me,

and I was trying to see it that way, too. Nose didn't have to hit me, and my table boys would have taken any reason to slug Nose. Still, I wished to hell they had put me on special force. I was glad, at least, that my face was still swollen.

I had to go back to my regular table, but I didn't know what I was going to say about why I wasn't put on force. Snicklesnort and Babybird were all sweaty and had straw stuck to their hair and clothes. They'd been throwing hay bales all day, but they were actually happy and proud and seemed to be looking to me for approval. It didn't seem to occur to them to ask why I got out of special force.

I was quiet while they told stories about the day. Then I said, "I'm sorry I got you guys in trouble." I was looking at the lacquered green wood of the table and my voice was choked up and weak.

Snicklesnort whined. "Don't be talking that shit, Professor. We got your back. And if that bastard comes after you again, we still got your back, special force or not." Babybird threw a couple punches in the air.

"Nose was just trying to look out for me," I said.

There was silence for a moment. Here these guys were being stand-up, being damned heroes, and I was pulling this sorry shit.

Finally, Snicklesnort laughed and shrugged as if to say, "What's with this guy?" Out loud he said,

"Yeah, Nose is looking out for you okay. He's looking out to shoot your cuff, man. You're going to have to get your shit together, Bowser. If you don't take him out, they're going to be coming at you next time. They're going to kill you." Just then we were called for showers.

The rest of the week, I couldn't stop thinking about Nose in lockdown and getting a six for progress. Then Saturday came around, and I was hanging out at my office under the tree. One white boy named Connor from another table came by just because he wanted to talk. He started off asking, "Professor, why do I wonder about things? I mean, I'm good with my hands. I could build a shed like that there just by looking at it, but why do I wonder about things?"

I said, "Connor, if you're good with your hands, you'll never want for anything." He acted like that was encouraging, but I had a feeling that he wasn't going to let them let him out, and if he did get out, he'd do something to get back in. "Connor, do they have you working at the brick shop?" I asked.

Connor looked sort of evasive, like he was ashamed of something. "No."

"Where are you working?"

"The infirmary. I got epilepsy. I guess they want me where they can keep an eye on me."

Then it occurred to me. "Connor, did you see Nose over in the infirmary?"

"Yeah," he said. "They got him locked down."

"Can you think of any way I could get in to see him?" I could see light come into Connor's eyes. It made perfect sense to him. I was going to use him to get at Nose while he was in the infirmary and hurt him. "Listen, Connor, I am not going to do anything that'll get you in trouble. I just want to see him and talk with him." Connor looked suspicious. "I'll give you a carton of cigarettes," I said.

That seemed to focus Connor's attention. "Can you get to the back door of the infirmary Monday afternoon at two?"

"Yeah, I think I can arrange that," I said.

Connor got very serious. "I don't know what you are up to, but you got to swear you ain't going to kill him, or even hurt him, while he's in the infirmary."

"I swear it, Connor. I just want to talk with him."

Monday, I went into the library as usual and tried to read, but I kept thinking about seeing Nose. At around one thirty, I got Miss Lovitt's permission to wander out to the stoop. I was going to risk taking off to the infirmary, even though I knew I would be in deep trouble if anyone thought I was trying to shoot the hump.

Then I saw Mr. Woodrow come in the door at the far end of the building, and I thought of a plan. I yelled down the hall, "Mr. Woodrow, sir, may I speak with you?" Mr. Woodrow didn't answer, but he leaned against the wall and waited for me to walk down to him.

"May I speak with you in private, sir?" Mr. Woodrow looked amused and walked with me to the boiler room and inside. "Mr. Woodrow, I guess you heard about Nose," I began.

"The way Mr. Palmer tell it, Nose's trying to kill him."

My blood was pounding. "I was there. The Nub walked up and kicked Nose straight in the ass while his hands were on his head. Nose just couldn't control himself and went at the Nub. That's when the son of a bitch clobbered him." Woodrow nodded slowly. I could tell he knew the Nub's story was a lie when he heard it. He just smiled and waited for me to say what I wanted.

"Sir, I want to go talk to Nose. Will you go with me?"

Mr. Woodrow's smile got bigger. "Damn, you get some ideas, don't you?"

"Connor, the infirmary boy, said he'd let me in the back door at two."

"Well, why'd he want to do that?" said Mr. Woodrow. "We was planning to go over to look at the condition of the paint anyways. I got the keys. You just go get Nose's jar and catch a hoppergrass to go in it. I'll go by and tell Miss Lovitt I need you to hep on some repairs at the infirmary."

We met outside on the stoop. Mr. Woodrow held the hoppergrass jar while I went for a ladder and some caulk. Then we walked over to the infirmary. Connor had been waiting by the inside of the back door. He was worried when he saw Mr. Woodrow let himself in, and amazed when he saw me following.

Mr. Woodrow shot him a big smile. "What you doing back here, boy? Guarding the back door? Expecting Injuns to attack?"

We walked through the big hall where everything was old and brick with big fans, like the dining hall, but very clean, with cots and partitions for Doc's exams and shots. Then we went back to the lock-down rooms and found Nose's, Connor following behind. When we got to Nose's room, Woodrow said to Connor, "You go on back to your chores. If Mr. Franklin comes back, you just tell him we caulking and sealing and checking for mildew." Connor walked off down the hall.

Nose was laying back with a bandage around his head, and when he heard Mr. Woodrow's key in the door, he popped up to a sitting position. He couldn't believe what he was seeing when we both came in. Mr. Woodrow looked very official. "We represent the department of maint'ance, and we been told you got some redecorating for us to do." Then he stroked his chin and looked around the tiny whitewashed block room, with a commode in the corner and grilles on the one window. "Not bad, Nose. I like what you done to the place, especially that commode. Louis VIII, ain't it? Nice touch. But I believe you need to *excessorize*. Yes, sir, *excessorize*. Mr. Bowser dog, did you bring along that Lois XVIII hoppergrass jar?" I handed it to Nose and we all cracked up laughing. I pulled out a pack of Camels and motioned to Mr. Woodrow to see if he thought it was cool if we smoked. Mr. Woodrow took the pack from me, pulled one out and lit it. "Don't you fret. I was in here inspecting, and when I inspect, I smoke. Nose, if Mr. Franklin asks you, you just go on and tell him that, and that he can talk to me." We all lit up and used the commode for an ashtray.

Nose was grinning at first, happy as hell to see us, but after a while he sort of remembered he had a bone to pick with me. "Bowser, why you got to be huffing a spot remover rag with them no-'count white boys? Who give it to you, Snicklesnort?"

"It was my idea, Nose," I said. Nose looked like he was disgusted and couldn't believe it.

"What the hell you want to be huffing that stuff for? To get high?"

"No, I got spots in my nose," I said. Nobody laughed. They both seemed embarrassed. "Listen, Nose. I just keep dreaming the same stuff, going back to the same stories and making them up over and over again, but nothing ever happens. We stay here, and the stories go around faster and faster until they spin, and they make me dizzy and I want to scream. I had to get out, even if it was just by making myself sick, to stop the stories for a minute."

We all sat quietly for a while after that and couldn't think of anything to say. Finally, Mr. Woodrow pulled out some Red Man, put a chaw in his mouth, and said, "Nose, I don't believe you ever finished telling us how you came to be here."

Nose lay back in his cot.

———

Like I told you, we got us about twenty ducks in pillowcases and met back up at the sign with the Jewish star on it. This time we went back across the street two at a time when no cars was coming. The tracks run down behind the fences on the back side of house lawns until they come to a road. Off to the right you can see through the trees a big lighted sign with a Scotch guy on it winking. We headed off through the woods in that direction, and when we got to the parking lot, I walked up to the pay phone outside and dialed the operator and told her, "Get me the police." I said to the man who answers at the police station, like I'm scared to death, "Robbery going down, Scotty Mart on Dupont by the train tracks."

Then I strolled on back to the woods, where all the

other boys was lying on their bellies watching for the cops to come. Seemed like only a minute before two cop cars come up, quiet with their lights off. One car went around to the back of the station. Two cops got out, drew their pistols, and covered the back door. The other car stopped on the side we was on, and two cops got out, drew their guns, and started to creep toward the front door.

One of the cops raised his head just enough to peek in the window, and watched for a long time. Finally, he seemed to kind of figure out that there wasn't no robbery, but both cops still went in, pistols first, each one holding his gun in two hands fixing to aim, just in case.

As soon as they both in the station, I say, "Go!" and two boys ran out, opened the back door of the cruiser, threw in two ducks, closed the door, and ran back. Then another two and another until that car was full of six quacking ducks.

Cops come around the corner. They could see something moving in the car and hear quacking. One of them opened the car door while the other held a gun on the door. Before the door was half open, ducks come flapping out at the cop with the gun. I guess one knocked his arm, because his gun went off and shot the Scotch guy on the sign right between the eyes.

When the cops inside the store heard the shot, they come running around the corner with their guns out, and the Indian guy from the store comes running out to see what's going on. Round that time me, Roberto, and eight other guys done creeped around in the woods to the other side of the store with the rest of the ducks. Pork George, still at the other end of the lot, stood up, stepped into the light of the parking lot, and yelled, "Hey, cops! Maybe you can shoot that little Scotty, but we faster! Then he and some boys took off and tore through the woods yelling "QUACK QUACK QUACK QUACK QUACK!"

Round that time the ducks was flapping out of the squad car and quacking all over the lot. All the cops walked over in the direction the boys run off. The store man was far away from the door out there with them.

I say, "Go!" and rushed the door with all the other boys. Each of us ran in, dropped a duck, grabbed a bottle of wine, and ran back out. The store man come back around the corner in time to see us run off, and yelled, "Stop!" We just kept going back around to the train tracks. The other five with Roberto circled back to the woods behind the station and waited for the cops to leave. Roberto told us later that the Indian was scream-ing at the cops about shooting the Scotty sign and tried to get them to help him clear the ducks out of his store, but the cops just drove away pissed off.

After that, the store man went back in the store, cussing to hisself, and started chasing ducks around. Roberto watched from the front window. By and by the Indian chased a duck into the storeroom, and that's when Roberto and four others ran into that store for another raid on the wine.

———

"So they nabbed you for stealing wine?" I asked.

And Nose said, "Hold on now. I ain't through yet."

———

By the time we got back to the tracks, there was a full moon and not a cloud passed across. We started to chugging wine and telling the story, each one of us telling it from where we saw it, and everybody jumping in and adding stuff. We couldn't be any happier about ourselves if we was all generals who just won a war. When it got to be about ten o'clock, Simple's little brother, Smiley, started to get sleepy.

"Hey, y'all, when we going home?" he asked.

"Yeah, we better go soon if we going to catch the bus," I said.

But Simple say, "Hold on just a minute. I still got a little wine left in this bottle."

We was all getting smoked. That's when we saw a light coming down the tracks. At first, everybody thought it was a car. It was pretty close when Pork George yelled out, *"TRAIN!"* We all up and started to run, but a few feet from the tracks I must've heard Smiley hollering above the train because I turned around to look and he was lying on the tracks in the full moonlight, crying. He must have tried to run, then tripped and got catched on something like a spike or a splintered tie.

I didn't think. I jumped just like a broad jump back on the tracks. I grabbed Smiley by the collar with both hands and pulled him loose and then pushed him down the hill. Somehow I ended up sitting straight up with the train *ON TOP OF ME!* All I could do was lay back on the ties. I knew I was dead then. I was in the dark and everything was blowing up, like a bomb that keeps blowing up and that don't stop. It just blew up, on and on. It felt like being in the middle of a bomb when it goes off. The ties I laid on shook and rattled under the weight. One single bump would throw me into that boom and it would grind me like meat. I could feel the wind from the axles in my face, and I knew it would just take a little loose piece to rip my face right off, and everything around me kept blowing up.

That's the last thing I remember until I came to. Cops and ambulance men was searching the tracks for what might be left of me.

When I opened my eyes, the cop leaning over looked to me like a angel. His eyes was wide and blue, and he say, "Great God almighty!"

———

Nose paused at that point. Mr. Woodrow sat ruminating for a minute, then spat a wad and said, "Nose, you know the Lord saved you to do something." I wondered if Nose believed that.

Finally Nose said quietly, but with conviction, "That's what I feel like. Like I already died and He sent me back for something."

We had to go back then, but I made Nose promise he'd tell me the rest of the story later. He said he would only if I promised to tell him how I got sent up. He wasn't buying the "victim of circumstance" line. He didn't even find it amusing.

Nose handed me the hoppergrass jar. "You better take this," he said.

"Don't you want to keep him here for company?" I asked. Nose pointed to the grille on the window. I took the jar and said I'd let the hoppergrass go outside.

Then Nose asked me, "You ever been to DC?"

I said, "Yeah, man." Nose was smiling that big crooked smile of his, with his eyes shining.

"Damn, Bowser, you my homeboy!"

· 7 ·

BLOOD AND BROWN CLOTH

EVAN'S FACE STILL LOOKED a mess, with one cheek swollen and both eyes black from his nose being broken, but they'd put him back on force. Snickle-snort and Babybird were still on force, along with Gray and Miles. Through supper, the boys talked mostly about treading. You got a boy from the other gang alone with your gang when Shorty Nub was not looking. Then you'd tread the boy—hit him and kick him until his gang showed up or Shorty Nub came back. The white boys caught Miles alone and roughed him up a little and threw him in a thorn patch. The black boys got Babybird and held him down and made him eat grass. Harmless hijinks. Nobody was getting hurt.

The first night Evan was back in the cottage, he and I were hanging out with the radio under the steps. They were playing "Both Sides Now" by Joni Mitchell. I said, "Man, you look like somebody took a tenderizer to your face."

Evan said, "You should see the other guy."

"Yeah, I did. He got clubbed good. Evan, listen, I'm sorry."

"What for? You didn't smack me. Nose did, and when he goes on force with us tomorrow maybe we'll give him another clubbing."

"Evan, Nose was not out to get me."

"You could have fooled me."

I still couldn't think of a good way to explain it. "I started it, and I didn't do a thing to help."

We listened to the radio for a minute, and Evan looked like he was working something out in his mind.

"I know you, boy. You'll get my back another time, and I've got yours."

Evan put his hand up at the angle of an arm wrestler, and I grasped his hand. That was the last I ever spoke with him.

Mr. Lindquist never did have me punished for the Carbona, although he never got over it either. Maybe they just added it to my loony file. I was worried about what it would do to Nose's progress. It looked certain that they were going to shoot him a six, at the very least, and they could do worse. I was truly sorry for that. As for my table boys, special force was a small price to pay for what the rumble did for their stories. If they were worried about how it would affect their progress, they didn't show it. Neither Nose nor my table boys were holding any grudge against me. The only ones who'd turned hostile about it were Miles and Gray, and that was because they were watching Nose's back. I think most of the boys were grateful that the Carbona incident gave them something to talk about.

Come Wednesday night, I went through the chow line with my hands in my back pockets and didn't see my table boys anywhere. Since Evan had told me Nose would be on force, I looked for him but didn't see him either. When I reached the end of the line, I saw Ben Susan alone at our usual table and started to head over to join him, but Mr. Lindquist came up and took my arm. "Why don't you join me this evening, Bowser."

It was just the two of us at the table, and Mr. Lindquist started by offering grace. "Dear merciful Lord, thank you for all of the blessings of this day. Take to your bosom those who have departed from us. Comfort those who grieve, and bless this food to the good of our bodies and our bodies and lives to your service, we humbly ask in the name of Christ Jesus, our Lord. Amen." Then Mr. Lindquist tried to ease into what he wanted to get at. He started with the food. "Okra and tomatoes—one of my favorite things about summer, just like my grandma used to put out in the summer when we'd visit, fresh from the garden." I didn't say anything. Finally he blurted it out. "Bowser, I got some bad news for you. There was an accident today on special force. They were pulling a stump out with the tractor, and . . . well . . . a boy got caught under the stump and was killed. It was Evan."

I didn't say anything, and Mr. Lindquist put down his knife and fork and leaned toward me. "Bowser, I know how close you and Evan were. I wanted to tell you before you heard it somewhere else, and I wanted you to know that I'm here to listen if you need me." I stared at Mr. Lindquist across the table.

"Who was driving the tractor?" I asked.

It was the first time I'd seen him off center. He took a slow bite of chicken to give him time to think. "Mr. Palmer was driving the tractor, Bowser, but it wasn't his fault. He yelled for the boys to stand clear, but Evan jumped back in the hole."

I kept staring. "Evan ain't stupid. Why'd he do that?"

I could see Mr. Lindquist's mood change like I'd tripped a switch. "For God's sake, Bowser, your best friend just died. Can't you think of anything but who to tag the blame on?"

I thought about that for a second, but all I felt was pissed off. "Shorty Nub is lying," I said.

That night I didn't sleep. I tried to grasp that Evan was dead, but I was not able to. Toward dawn, thoughts turned from him to me. It seemed, horribly, that I knew this place. I was back here where a friend dies because of me—because I set him up and didn't do a thing to stop it.

Next morning, we were in line for breakfast, and Babybird came in behind me and he started whispering really fast, "Did you hear about Evan?"

"Yeah," I whispered. "Tell me what happened."

"Mr. Greenjeans drove up in his pickup truck while we was in the field. He called to Shorty Nub, and the Nub put Snicklesnort in charge and went away with Greenjeans." I saw that Babybird's eyes weren't right.

I asked, "Babybird, are you okay?"

"They been giving us pills to keep calm—"

Snicklesnort broke line and came and shoved Babybird and told him, "Shut up."

Babybird looked confused but managed to answer back, "But I'm just talking to Bowser. He ain't going to tell nobody."

"You're still high. You don't know what the fuck happened. Shut up!" Snicklesnort told him.

Shorty Nub walked over and pulled both of them out of line, gently for the Nub. He took them aside out of hearing distance. I could see Snickle talking and Babybird hanging his head. Then the Nub reached over and took Babybird by the arm and said something in his ear. It looked like Babybird was protesting, making an excuse. Shorty Nub put his hand over Babybird's mouth and put his arm around his shoulders. Then all three of them were not talking, and Shorty Nub led the two boys away toward the infirmary.

That night at the cottage, I pumped Babybird and Snicklesnort, but they told it just as Mr. Lindquist had. I said to Babybird, "Well, how could Shorty Nub have been driving the tractor if he went off with Mr. Greenjeans like you said?"

Babybird was flustered. "I was high when I said that."

Snicklesnort wasn't flustered. "If Babybird said Shorty Nub went off with Mr. Greenjeans, he was right. But the Nub came back *before* the accident."

I didn't say anything, but I wondered why Babybird was trying to take back what he'd said if it was true. I saw Nose over at the water fountain and went to talk with him. Gray and Miles were watching, ready to jump me if I started anything. "Nose," I asked, "what happened?"

All he would say was "I don't know what happened, man. Leave me alone."

The next day at the library, I pulled into Nose's office. I opened the door and saw him for a moment before he saw me, in the light of the single bare bulb. Nose was sitting on one of the wooden school chairs, looking just like a scared little kid. He was holding the jar with the hoppergrass and staring at it. When he heard me, he jerked his head up and just looked.

"How were those pills, man?" I asked him.

Nose laughed. "Homeboy, we was stoned."

"What were they?" I asked.

"Felt like I-don't-give-a-damn pills."

"You got to go back on force?" I asked.

"No, man." Nose smiled. "We all traumatized."

I pulled out a couple Camels and we smoked them. I waited for Nose to tell me about Evan, but he wouldn't. Finally I got tired of waiting. "Come on, man, what the hell happened?"

Nose wouldn't look at me, and he didn't say anything for a long time. Then he did look at me, really serious. "Bowser, I ain't supposed to be telling this to nobody, and if you tell anyone I told you, my ass will be fried."

"I won't," I said.

Nose loosened up a little. "Shorty Nub telling me

to tell the story a way it didn't happen. He say if I don't, he can say that I did it, and I could get tried as an adult and get locked up for good."

"Did what? Mr. Lindquist told me it was an accident."

Nose started looking jumpy again. He was looking all over the place but not at me. Then he looked at the door for a while and finally pulled his chair up in front of me and looked wild in my face.

"I'm going to tell you what happened now." Then he was wagging his finger in my face. "Don't you dare tell nobody—not your homeboys, not even your mumma."

"I won't," I promised. And Nose told it like this.

The Nub take us out to pull up a stump. He pulled with the big Massey, and we pushed from behind and hepped to guide it. That simple white bastard with the overalls come up, and Shorty Nub go off with him. He leave Snicklesnort in charge, and he leave a cooler of water for us, but it was hot with no shade.

So we was out there in the sun, hot as shit, not doing nothing. Miles go, "This is stupid. Shorty Nub might be gone all day. I'm going over to that big oak and get out of the sun."

Snicklesnort say, "Yeah, you go on and do that. You

just go ahead and do that, and the Nub will whip your ass when he see you run off."

Gray say, "Not if I say I going to tell on him going off and getting smoked, he ain't."

Snickle say, "The Nub even hears you been talking that way and he make you wish you was dead."

Everybody shut up then, because they knowed Snickle was right. Even if we all ratted on Shorty Nub, they'd nobody believe us, and the Nub would get whoever talked and mess them up good.

Babybird say, "Snickle, we can't just sit out here and roast like pigs. What the hell do you suggest?"

Snickle thought for a while. Then he say, "Listen, y'all help me get this stump out of here. If we get that done while he gone, it will cover his ass and I bet I can get him to lay off us for leaving the tractor." Everybody seen Snickle run the tractor for mowing before, and we couldn't stand just sitting there in the sun doing nothing, so we all jumped in.

When the Nub walked off, the tree was lying on its side and cut down to the ball of roots and about four foot of trunk. We already dug all around it and cut the big roots, and Shorty pulled the tree over with chains.

We took the chains off and wrapped them around the part of the root-ball that was sticking out of the ground, then hooked up the chains to the tractor. When Snickle gunned the Massey and put her in gear, that root-ball pulled right out of there at first, but then she stuck on something. That big chained hunk of dirt and roots was halfway up out of the hole, and it stuck there. So Evan say, "Let's break this mother loose so we can get out of here." Him and me jumped down in the hole with axes to cut the roots loose where they's hung up.

Evan spotted where a root was still holding, and he go right under the big part of the root-ball and reached up to get at it. Just then the chain slipped and the trunk come down to the side and trapped Evan's arm and he screaming, man. Babybird was up top just screaming and waving his hands for Snicklesnort to pull the stump off Evan, but when Snickle pulled forward, the stump didn't come up—she pulled sideways. I heard Evan's bones of his shoulder, and I screamed, "Let her back!" I hoped it would twist back off him, but it didn't. The chains slipped loose all the way. I saw them come loose and just jumped free before the trunk fall flat down on the poor boy and twist around on him, and he didn't scream no more.

We didn't know what to do. Snickle jumped off the tractor. He was crying and running around looking for a place to wrap the chain, but he couldn't find one. Miles and Gray tried to use their own weight to lever the trunk, but it did not budge. Babybird say, "I'm running for help," and he started off for the road, but before he got there, Shorty Nub showed back up. He wasn't smoked. Everybody was yelling at him at the same time, trying to tell him what happened. Babybird screamed, "We got to get him out of there!" but the Nub seemed to get harder than ever.

"SHUT UP!" he yelled. The Nub walked over to the hole and studied it. You couldn't see nothing of Evan except his one arm bended around like a pretzel. All the rest of him was under that root-ball. The Nub studied the chains and hooked them around the best he could. Then he get on the Massey and gunned her. That root twist around and take Evan's arm back under it, then the root seemed to pull up, and we could see Evan just like a big bunch of bloody clothes, and his leg was twisted up and his arm was like a pretzel and almost cut off. Then the root fall flat on him again.

It was the third try before the Nub get the root pulled out of the hole. By that time Evan was facedown, and his body was just mash and blood and brown cloth. Shorty Nub go down in the hole like he going to take Evan's pulse or feel his throat, but Evan was so mashed up that the Nub couldn't find nothing like a wrist or a throat, and he just crawled right back out.

Then he say, "Y'all listen to me. We can't do nothing about Evan. It's too late, but we got to stick together on this if we going to get through it."

The way he said it made us all think for the first time that we could get in a pile of trouble. The Nub say, "You know you boys wasn't supposed to be messing with this tractor. I'm afraid they could blame you all for this

102

boy's death." Then he didn't say nothing for a long time . . . until it looked like something come to him. "I think I can get us out of this, but y'all got to play along real close. This is what happened: I was driving the Massey, see? And I told y'all to stay clear of the hole. Then the stump hanged up, and I yelled, 'Stay back,' but Evan didn't listen. He grabbed the ax and jumped down the hole and tried to cut loose that root hisself. He ended up knocking the chain loose at the same time, and the next thing we know, the stump is down on him and he gone.

"Now y'all boys can go with this story, or we can march right down and say that y'all took it on yourselves to play with the tractor when you was supposed to wait for me to get back with supplies, and you done killed a boy. It's up to you."

Snicklesnort was crying, and he say, "It was hot as shit out here, Mr. Palmer. We just wanted to get your work done on this stump so we could get out of the sun."

The Nub put his hand on Snickle's shoulder like he was his daddy, and he say, "I know y'all didn't mean no harm. Y'all are good boys. You just tell it like I said it, and we'll get along past this whole thing." Then he made us all swear that we'd tell it just that way and wouldn't budge, and that if anyone told anything different to any-body, we was to tell him about it.

I said, "So Shorty Nub doesn't want anybody to know he went off and left the boys on special force."

"You got it," said Nose.

———

Shorty Nub packed us up in his truck, but this time he tell Snicklesnort to stay with the boys in back, and he tell me to ride in the cab. The other boys was still so shook up that they hardly noticed how strange it was for the Nub to let a black boy ride with him.

As soon as I was up in the cab, the Nub say, "You don't hold nothing against me for tapping you on the head now, do you?"

So I say, "Why don't you let me knock you upside the head like that and tell me if it's a tap?"

The Nub smiled, the way he does when he's about to smack somebody, and he say, "Are you threatening me, boy?" I didn't say nothing. "Let's cut the small talk," he say. "Why don't you tell me where you was when that root come down on Evan?" I still didn't say nothing. He say, "The way the other boys just told it, you was the only one in the hole with Evan, and you jumped out right before she crushed him."

"Yeah, so?" I say.

"Well, that could look pretty bad, couldn't it?" he say.

"What do you mean?" I ask him.

"Let's see now. You was in a fight with Evan and get your head broke and put on force. So you waited until he was down in the hole with you, and you take your ax to the chain and jump out right before it fall on him all the way."

"What the hell you talking about?" I ask.

"Once they get calmed down, the white boys might remember seeing it happen just like that," he say. "Then you wouldn't be looking at progress at all. No sirree. Then you talking about manslaughter. We could get you charged as an adult and maybe you never see the outside of a prison."

"I ain't killed him," I told him. "If you hadn't run off, he probably still be alive."

"Now there's where you have to be very careful, boy," he say. "Very careful. There's a way out of this, but that ain't the direction. But if you want to play it that way, my word against yours, we'll see whose side the white boys'll take, that's okay with me. Remember, it don't look good if they take it on theyselves to pull with a tractor and kill a boy. Is that the way you want to play it?"

"What do you want me to do?" I ask him.

"You just stick with the story, is all," he say. "I was driving the tractor and told y'all to stand back. You heared Evan say, 'I had enough of this standing in the sun,' and he jumped down the hole with the ax and started to flailing at the root. Then Snickle yelled at me that Evan was in the hole, and when I let off the torque, everything commenced to happen just the way you saw it. Well, what do you say? You going to go with the rest of us or not?"

I couldn't think of no way out. "Yeah, I'll go along," I say.

"That's the boy," the Nub say. "Just remember, if anybody hears a different story, I'm going to know it come from you, and I'll see you never get free. You know I can do that."

Then he starts getting goofy. He go, "I can do it because I got the *power*. This one's *iron* and this one's *steel,* and if the left one don't get you, the right one *weel."* Then he starts to laugh at himself, and the son of a bitch winks at me!

———

"What do you think, Professor? What would you do?"

I hated Shorty Nub so badly, I wanted to feel his throat in my hands. My first reaction was to tell Nose to just tell the truth, but then I thought about what that would mean to Nose.

"If you want to get out of here, Nose," I said, "I'd say you must go with that story. The Nub can mess you up if you go against him."

· 8 ·

ASYLUM

ON SUNDAY MORNINGS we were marched to chapel.
Each week we had a guest chaplain. This time it was
the Reverend Bacon. As soon as Mr. Ball introduced
him, a few of the boys started to make grunting hog
sounds. It was hot and the Reverend Bacon had
sweat all over his face. He tried to be down-homey,
but it was clear that he was not having a good time.

He started off by asking us, "D'y'all see that
advertisement on TV for Corn Huskers Lotion?" We
didn't have TVs in the cottages. "They tell you, 'Try
Corn Huskers Lotion. It works!' Well, boys, I'm here
to tell you this morning, Try Jesus. He works!"

I think he could tell he wasn't pulling any drag, so
he switched gears and got personal. "Boys, I know
how it is to be down like you. I was a drunk and a
sinner before the Lord reached down to pick me up."

Miles was sitting up in his pew, tall and solemn with his arms crossed, like a judge. He yelled out in his deep, adult voice, "I don't care to hear it!" Mr. Ball shot him a dirty look, but that's all. I think Mr. Lindquist was smiling.

After the sermon, Mr. Pope stood up. Mr. Pope was a little guy whose blond hair looked like it was molded in place. He worked at a local church and volunteered on the Hill. Usually his face looked like he had sour stomach, and he was peevish to anyone who wasn't doing his music. Today, though, he was introducing like Liberace. "Boys, we have a special treat for you this morning. Our own King's Men! They've been working hard on this piece, and I know you'll enjoy it."

Three guys from Cottage D huddled around in front of the chapel. One of them played chords on a guitar, and they sang a folk song called "I Walk the King's Highway" in manly low voices with their brows furrowed. I think everybody liked it, though you wouldn't catch anybody saying so. I kept waiting for the preacher or Mr. Ball or somebody to say something about Evan, but they never did.

Back at the cottage, I went to my locker to get a pack of fogs. In Evan's compartment there was the package of little white Hostess doughnuts, the carton of Marlboros, the shoe box, and the radio/cassette player. I took out the little picture book with the Eiffel

Tower on it, and I opened it to pictures of Constance. I had to tell myself Evan wasn't here anymore. Otherwise, it was easy for him to never have been here. I guess his mom and Constance had a service for him in Fredericksburg, but anything about him being on the Hill sure wasn't going to be talked about—ever.

Then me and Snickle and Babybird and Ben Susan were sitting around the table smoking and not looking at one another. Evan's chair was empty. Finally, Snicklesnort looked up and whined, "Bowser, give me Evan's fogs, man. You already got plenty." I could feel the empty space on the chair next to me where Evan should have been, and I looked down so the other boys couldn't see if I started to blubber.

Evan sacrificed himself. Although he never actually said it, I had a feeling that he'd been selling the drugs and saving up money because he dreamed of getting his sister away from home. And when he went to special force where he would be killed, it was because he stood up to protect me.

That night in line for the dorm, Gray shouted behind me, "Bowser, give me Evan's doughnuts, man."

I got out of line in my underwear and turned around to everybody. "What do you think I should do with Evan's stuff? You want me to divide it up and give it to you all? Well, fuck you. It's all mine!" I walked over to my locker.

Mr. Lindquist was halfway up the stairs with boys in his way. He didn't see me break line until I was at the locker. "Fall in, Bowser!" he hollered.

I opened the locker and took out the carton of cigarettes, opened it, and started taking out handfuls of the smokes and shoving them in my mouth. I took the little white doughnuts and shoved them in my mouth with the cigarettes. Then I chewed, swallowed, gagged, and put more cigarettes and more doughnuts in my mouth. Mr. Lindquist was yelling at me to fall back in, and I kept eating and gagging. When Mr. Lindquist was next to me shaking me, I grabbed the Eiffel Tower photo album and started tearing out pages and ripping them up as fast as I could. Then I fell to my knees, puking tobacco and doughnuts, ripping at the pictures with both hands. Vomit was mixing up with little pieces of Constance.

After Mr. Ball took me to the infirmary, I lost track of things for a while. The next I can remember, I was lying on a cot with clean white sheets in a brick hall with a very high ceiling. There were fans on the ceiling and two rows of empty cots. I was sure this place had been a hospital a long time ago, in the Civil War. I could imagine a soldier, face black from powder, waiting for the knife. I could imagine the screams worn into the bricks like soot. I wanted to scream but did not.

Evan didn't seem so much dead as not alive. He

was an unalive character in the Nub's story. I was undead, like a vampire in a movie, and all the other boys weren't alive or dead. Nothing we did or thought or said meant anything at all. What happened in Hill time was just to measure when we might go away. Story time was a drug that we used to pretend we were alive. I imagined looking at the boys around me, and I hated them for being unalive, and I hated them more for seeing that I wasn't alive. Evan wasn't dead. The boys who saw him die got drugged to make his death not have happened. His dying turned into an alibi for Shorty Nub.

Before I drifted off, I heard Mr. Franklin, the clinic man, say to Mr. Ball, "That shot should do it. As soon as he's out, we'll lock him down."

Lockdown was where they put you if you shouldn't or couldn't be around the other boys for any reason. Sometimes a hardrock would end up there on his way to Lorton, the maximum security facility. Sometimes they'd put a boy with the flu in there.

I woke up woozy, with the events of the night before seeming a little scary but somehow amusing, too—like a comedy nightmare. Light was streaming in the window, and the room was very clean; I felt a strange sense of well-being. After I played through the story, there was nothing else to do, so I kept going over all the events, starting from Mr. Lindquist telling me Evan had been killed.

Each time the story got faster, and each time the idea of Evan being undead and the rest of us being undead wore deeper and deeper—and proved itself more each time around. Connor came with breakfast: half of a piece of toast, half a scrambled egg, half a sausage patty. The staff in the dining hall always cut the portions on their own to punish anyone in lockdown.

I was used to eating the same amount at every meal and every meal coming at the same time. It was now nine o'clock, and the half portions made everything seem wrong. I began to feel afraid of my own fear of things being wrong, and I kept going back to Evan, replaying what really happened and trying to hold on to it. I found myself trying to picture what his corpse looked like, all mashed up. Then my mind wandered back to Huckleberry Finn and Jim finding Pap's body in the house floating down the flooded river in the storm. That flowed into story time and something I remembered. Bradley Davis, Audrey, a black boy named Wolfe, and I were swinging from a rope swing and swimming in the river. A storm was blowing up, but we were having a good time for a while. Then the sky was black and there was a crack of lightning in the dark, and I heard Bradley yell, "Where's Wolfe?"

Then, through the lightning cracks and the thunder and the hard rain, the yelling, "Where's Wolfe?"

He wasn't anywhere. Somehow we ended up staggering to the nearest house in the rain. The lady there wouldn't let us in and called the police. When they arrived, we told them that Wolfe had drowned.

Later one of us had the idea that we should go over and talk to Wolfe's mom and dad. His family lived in a block of Jefferson Village that I had never been to before. Sometimes we'd go to the Winn-Dixie in that neighborhood and wait in the alley next to it to pay a wino a buck fifty to get us a seventy-nine-cent bottle of wine. But the people who lived around there seemed as far away as Africa to me.

We knocked on the door, and Wolfe's father came and stood there in an undershirt with no sleeves. He'd been crying, but his broad, scarred, black face was blank now. He didn't invite us in the door. You could smell kitchen smells from the stoop, and they smelled different from white kitchen smells. He said, "The police say they planning to dredge for my boy's body. I don't know if I want to see my son all bloated and gray."

It turned out Wolfe hadn't drowned at all. We were all so stoned we just lost him. Somehow he walked off and met up with some people and went and partied with them. He turned up late that night, but I don't remember exactly what happened. I was high the whole time and it was all blurry.

For just a moment I thought maybe that would

happen with Evan. Maybe he was alive somewhere and they would find him. It didn't take much thinking, though, to know that this was different. This time the only thing left of Evan was a mangled corpse.

On day two, Connor came in with breakfast, and Mr. Franklin opened the door. I started going at the Evan story again; then I drifted into story time, riding my motorcycle; then I went back to the Evan story. It was so quiet.

Finally I heard loud voices down the hall. Nose was being dragged in by Shorty Nub and Mr. Ball. They threw him in the lockdown room down the hall. After the door closed, I could hear the Nub say, "Mean, evil-looking boy." Mr. Ball said, "They'll know how to care for him."

After their footsteps disappeared, I went to the door and kicked it and yelled out, *"Nose."*

He yelled back, *"Bowser."*

And me: *"What you doing here?"*

Nose: *"I don't know, man. They started askin' me questions yesterday after breakfast. Then today they carried me here."*

It was hard work shouting down the hall, and anyone could hear, so we quit. When Connor came by with Mr. Franklin to give me lunch, I caught Connor on the way out and whispered, "I got to talk to you, man. Come back around." He nodded, but I didn't know whether I'd see him or not. I couldn't get to my fogs or anything to favor him with. Finally, he did come around.

"Listen, Connor, I need to know why Nose is in here. Did you hear anything?"

Connor said, "All I know is after they brought him in I overheard Mr. Ball and the Nub talking about sending him down to Lorton."

I said, "Connor, do this for me. Tonight, when you go to dinner, sit next to Ben Susan. Find out what he knows. It'll be worth a carton of fogs, brand of your choice."

"I'll try," he said.

"One other thing," I said. "I need something to read or I'll go nuts. Can you give me anything?"

"All we got is Bibles."

"Get me one, will you?"

Connor came back around with a Bible and gave it to me. In lockdown, Hill time grinds so slow it's torture and story time can spin so fast you get dizzy. I kept going over things until it got to me; then I'd try to read some. It was very hard reading. I tried to start from the beginning but got lost. I tried at the beginning of the New Testament, but I couldn't get past the "begats."

Finally, I tried Psalms. I didn't get any traction there either, until I got to Psalm 7, and those first lines stuck.

O Lord my God, in thee do I take refuge;
save me from all my pursuers, and deliver me,
lest like a lion they rend me, dragging me away,
with none to rescue.

I tucked away the psalm in my memory and recited it to myself now and then.

Next day, Connor came back around with the news from Ben Susan.

***

Ben Susan says Nose got questioned by somebody from the state and screwed the pooch. They caught him lying about Evan getting mashed. When the Nub found out, he got word through Snicklesnort to the white boys who were there. He told them to change the story, that Nose chopped that root down on Evan on purpose and that they been covering for Nose, and the Nub never knew about it. Mr. Lindquist told Ben Susan that they didn't want to call a lot of attention to Evan's death by actually charging Nose, so they were going to send him down to Lorton for being uncontrollable.

***

"Did they tell this to Nose?" I asked.

"No. He don't know nothing."

"Connor, go over and talk to Nose and find out

what went on—what they asked him, and what he told them."

Connor looked very suspicious. "Why the hell do you care? That black bastard would kill you if he got the chance. What are you after? Are you still out to get that boy?"

"I'm only trying to piece the crime together," I said. "Like Mike Hammer. Why don't you work with me on this one and try to figure out what really happened? Maybe when we're done, we can write a crime story and get it published." I could tell Connor was trying to be cool about it, but he was hooked. Infirmary duty must be boring most of the time, and he liked the idea of being a detective and writing a crime story.

When Connor came back around, he told it like this:

———

They pulled Nose out of line after breakfast and took him to the Intake Cottage. There was some guy from Juvenile Corrections there. Nose said he was nice and smooth to Nose, and gave him cigarettes and sodas while they talked. He asked Nose to tell him what happened the day Evan died, and Nose told it like everybody has been telling it.

Then the man asked him, "Why do you think Evan jumped in that hole even after Mr. Palmer yelled for everybody to stand clear?"

Nose couldn't think of any good reason and said, "He just didn't want to mind."

And the man asked, "Was Evan hotheaded like that, to do something crazy just because he'd been told not to?"

Nose started to squirm, because anybody would have told the man that Evan wasn't like that a bit. So he said, "No, sir, he wasn't like that most times."

The man asked him again, "So why do you think Evan jumped in that hole with an ax after Mr. Palmer told him to stand clear?"

"Now I think about it, sir," Nose said, "I believe Evan was going in there after something. Yeah, something he might have dropped."

"Well, James," said the man, "you were standing there next to him. Didn't you see what he was going in after?"

"Yes, sir," said Nose. "I believe that was a pen he was going after. Yes, sir, a silver colored pen from his home." Well, as Nose was telling me about it, I know *he* knew that they'd find out whether that was true or not. If Evan had dropped a pen down there, they'd have found it. And if Evan had even owned a pen like that, Mr. Lindquist would know it.

After Connor left, I tried to digest it. I wanted to get the story straight and tell it.

I yelled, "Nose!" And he yelled back. I yelled, "Steady, man. Stay steady. You hear me?"

And Nose yelled like I never heard a person yell. Half moan and half scream, and there was nothing more to say.

It didn't take much reckoning to figure what the Nub was up to. Once they caught Nose in that lie, it'd be easy for the boys to push the Nub's story. Pinning the blame on Nose was better than saying it was an accident. By having Nose sent off to Lorton for being incorrigible, Shorty Nub would manage to shift attention from himself, keep them from investigating the accident any further, and get rid of Nose before he could convince anyone of the truth.

Meanwhile, Shorty Nub was covered all around: The boys were tangled up more in Shorty Nub's story and had a greater stake in keeping to it. Hill staff must have thought the Nub was being slack with Nose, since he wasn't saying that Nose should be investigated for murder or manslaughter. Everyone was happy. Everyone except Evan, who was dead, and Nose, who would be as good as. Evan's death had been mangled and distorted, like his body, and made unreal. Now Nose had been pulled into this freak show, like some punk called up on stage to be contorted into a box, then gone.

Next morning, Mr. Franklin came by after breakfast to take me to the rehab lab to meet with Mr. Silver. It was roasting, but I was happy to be outside walking across the courtyard, and I was busting to tell Mr. Silver what was really going on, to get the story straight. The rehab lab was in a trailer behind the school and Mr. Silver was waiting for me behind a shiny desk in the bright room. I took a seat on an orange plastic chair in front of him. Mr. Silver looked at me and shook his head. "Bowser, what the hell are you up to?"

"Listen, Mr. Silver, they're sending Nose to Lorton, but he didn't do anything."

"Nose? Are you talking about James Braxton?"

"Yeah."

"I don't see why that should concern you."

"Mr. Silver, he did not kill Evan."

Mr. Silver looked at me, amazed. I could see him thinking, "This boy really is insane." He said, "As far as I know, no one has accused James of killing anyone. Beyond that, I will not discuss his case with you. Let's talk about your case."

The blood in my head began pounding, and I could not speak. I felt like an idiot. I had thought, somehow, that all I needed to do was to get the story right and tell it. But this truth was a glowing hot coal and no one would touch it.

He kept talking to me, asking questions. I stopped listening until, finally, he said, "I need for you to talk to me, Richard. I'm concerned about you."

I jumped up and threw the orange plastic chair against the wall and said, "You can take your concern and shove it up your ass."

Back in lockdown I felt like I was drowning in mendacity, neither dead nor alive. I thought of the finger game they play with kids: "Here is the church. Here is the steeple. Open the doors and see all the people."

All they are is fingers, I thought, and all you can do with them is jerk off.

I was looking over to where there was no action, no consequence—where I was a victim of circumstance. On the street this was right about the point where I would start to binge: no church, no steeple, no people. I was over the edge, groping for a toehold or a fingerhold, with the feel of falling, the feel of distance below.

> O Lord my God, in thee do I take refuge;
> save me from all my pursuers, and deliver me,
> lest like a lion they rend me, dragging me away,
> with none to rescue.

Did I fall asleep praying those lines, or was I awake? "O Lord my God, in thee do I take refuge." There is a cave in the rock where you can take refuge. In the rock: "Rock of ages, cleft for me. Let me hide myself in Thee." I wanted to grab hold of that cleft and to hold on for my life. I wanted to crawl into that cave and hide myself in that refuge.

Next morning, they escorted me to the Intake Cottage to meet with the shrink. It was hot again, but there was a breeze. They took me to a room that must have been a director's office, with fake mahogany and paintings on the wall. Dr. Garcia greeted me. "Would you like a cigarette? A cigar?"

I had the feeling that each of these questions was a test. "Yes, a cigarette, please. I haven't had one since they locked me down. Inhumane if you ask me." He gave me a Marlboro. I took the cigarette and opened my mouth wide, like I was going to eat it. Then I closed my teeth on the filter, bit it off, and spit the filter into the trash basket. "I like my smoke." I smiled.

"So, you have been busy since Dr. Bruce saw you at the Diagnostic Center. Reading a lot, I hear. What have you been reading?"

"Twain, Steinbeck, Conrad, Thoreau, Frost."

"And eating cigarettes and doughnuts? Do you want to tell me about that?"

"Not much to tell. I just had an urge for a snack before bed. Right now I'm in the mood for jalapeños and ice cream. Maybe I'm pregnant."

"And inhaling spot remover. What is that for? To get high?"

"No, doctor. To tell you the truth, I got spots in my nose."

Dr. Garcia said, "Yes, yes, spots in your nose." He was looking at his notes, and I figured Mr. Lindquist had already quoted that line to him. "Why don't you tell me about Evan's death?"

I didn't answer, and he stopped. He didn't say

anything at all, just sat there. At first I thought it'd be fun to wait him out. I finished my cigarette and asked for another, bit the filter off, smoked it. I asked for another and asked, "Do you get paid by the hour?"

"I do, in fact," he said.

I asked to go to the toilet, and he walked me to the door, acting as though he was not worried about what I would do in there. I thought of what I might do in there, but all I could think of was breaking something—not my style. I figured Dr. Garcia knew that, which made me take him a little more seriously.

Back in the room, I studied an oil painting on the wall. In the foreground the simple white shape of a dog in motion brought the soft browns, greens, grays of hills behind to a point of focus. After biting filters off a couple more cigarettes, I asked, "How long am I going to be locked down?"

"I don't decide that. Are you ready to go back to the cottage?"

"I never asked to leave the cottage. I don't even know why they locked me down."

"You were vomiting? You were destroying property? Perhaps Mr. Lindquist thought that you would hurt yourself."

I gave him my best psychotic smile and mimicked the doctor's Latin accent. "Perhaps Mr. Lindquist thought that I would hurt someone else?"

Dr. Garcia shrugged. "Perhaps."

"Okay. Yeah, I'm ready to go back to the cottage. I won't hurt myself. I won't hurt anyone else."

"Richard, I see in your file that there is a plan to send you to a hospital, the St. George Asylum." He said the words very slowly and deliberately, not emphasizing the last word but letting it lie there at the end.

I smiled again. "They got girls there?"

He continued to stare at me with no expression. "You have been diagnosed a schizophrenic. The doctors at the hospital say that in cases like yours they recommend a commitment of indefinite duration. Although it is a very expensive institution, your father has agreed to make that commitment, because he loves you and is worried about you." He looked at his notes. "You are now fifteen?"

I wanted to get away from him—to lockdown, to the cottage, anywhere. "I just want out," I said softly.

Dr. Garcia continued. "I spoke to Mr. Silver, to Mr. Lindquist, and to Miss Lovitt, and they do not describe your behavior necessarily as that of a schizophrenic."

"I JUST WANT OUT!"

"Calm down, Richard. Calm down," he said.

I began to tell myself, Don't try to figure anything out now. Just get back to the cottage.

After a few moments of smoking in silence, I was able to regroup. "I'm calm, doctor. Shoot me another cigarette, will you? Do me a favor—bring Camels next time." Then after a few more drags, "I don't know what to think. I could be schizoid or I could be saner than you. But I know that if you let me go back to the cottage, I'll be able to think more clearly. If I'm not crazy now, I bet I will be if they keep me locked down much longer."

"Richard, before I can recommend that you go back to the cottage, you are going to have to talk to me about your friend dying and how you feel. Sad? Angry? Sometimes we need to let ourselves grieve, even cry."

"Listen. You want to talk about Evan dying? I know what happened. The crew boss left the hill. Evan was killed by accident while Mr. Palmer was gone. Mr. Palmer doesn't want anyone to know he left his post. My guess is he doesn't want anyone to know where he went or what he did, either. Now they're pinning it on Nose and sending him away quietly so no one will ask questions."

Dr. Garcia looked at me like he was trying to see where to fit a replacement part on something broken.

"Who's Nose?"

"Black boy. Works with me at the school. His real name is James Braxton."

"Richard, were you there when all this happened?"

"No. Plus, I was eating cigarettes. Plus, I'm diagnosed loony. I know nobody's going to believe me. But it's the truth, damn it. It's the truth."

· 9 ·

A BIRD IN THE HAND

BY DINNERTIME the next day, they let me join my cottage for supper. Snicklesnort and Babybird were happy to see me.

"They give you any good pills?" Snicklesnort asked.

"Better. They gave me a shot to put me out. It felt like smack's little brother. They stuck Nose in near me yesterday. What's going on there?"

Snicklesnort said, "We covered for that boy long enough, man. You know he killed Evan."

"So Nose killed Evan," I said.

"Yeah, he pushed him right in the damn hole and then he chopped that chain loose and jumped free."

"Pretty slick," I said. "Why do you think he did it?"

Snicklesnort answered, "You know better than

126

anybody. When Nose went after you, Evan stepped in for you. I don't know how you got off being on force, but the closest Nose could get to killing you was getting your locker mate."

Babybird chimed in, "Yeah, Bowser, how'd you get out of doing force, anyway?"

"Well, you know, they think I'm crazy," I said. I'd had enough. "You guys are absolutely full of shit. I don't even know why I'm trying to talk to you. You guys are nothing; you don't even exist. You aren't even alive. You're just characters in some bullshit story that Shorty Nub made up to cover his ass."

Snicklesnort said, "What the hell are you talking about, you crazy son of a bitch?" He was furious and I was losing it myself.

"I'm talking about your story being pure horse-shit," I said. "I'm talking about Shorty Nub leaving you in charge, and you driving the tractor when Evan was killed, and you all spinning these lies to hang it on Nose to cover the Nub."

The veins on Snickle's neck were sticking out. He was trying to whisper, but his voice was hissing out like a snake. "Evan's dead because he stuck up for you. We could get time for it all because we stuck up for you against that black bastard, and now you going to stand up for Nose against us? You weren't even there, Bowser. Plus, you are crazy as shit. What do you even have to say about it?"

Back at the cottage, Gray came up to me, took me by the throat, and held me against the lockers. "Our boy Nose go to Lorton and you dead." All the boys from my table just watched and looked away. Mr. Lindquist broke it up, but even he didn't seem to much care.

That night as we lined up for showers, Snicklesnort leaned from behind me and whispered, "You better think about whose side you going to be on. This is a tough cottage for a boy with no friends."

The next morning at breakfast, I tried to sit with my table, but Snicklesnort barred my way. "That seat's taken."

I walked around to a seat out of his reach, next to Babybird. "Listen to me," I said.

"Why would we want to hear anything you say, you fucking mad dog?" Snicklesnort said.

I tried to plead with him. "You are all just covering for Shorty Nub. Evan's dying is nobody's fault, except maybe Shorty Nub's. It was an accident, damn it! The only way this is going to get right is for you guys to tell it like it really happened. You did the best you could, Snickle. It wasn't your fault."

Snicklesnort was hissing again. "And since you weren't there, and you're out of your mind, why exactly do we need you to tell us what happened? Evan is dead, and those black boys would like to pin it on me. I know I didn't do it, and I ain't covering for

Nose. Nose has been out to get you from the start, and he had every reason to whack Evan, because Evan was your homeboy."

I shook my head. "What you said did not happen. Evan died from an accident that was allowed to happen because Shorty Nub left his post. Nose was not out to get me. He was my homeboy at work. When he saw me huffing the spot remover, he hit me because he wanted me to stop. Evan really lived—he is not just some character in your story—and he really died by an accident. Get real, guys. Get alive or get dead."

Snickle said, "So let me tell you what's happening. You are a psycho, huffing spot remover, eating cigarettes, tearing up pictures, talking some loony shit about not being alive. And you're telling us, who actually saw Evan die, what happened, when you weren't anywhere around when it happened, and you are calling us liars."

Then Babybird: "Cut it out, Bowser. Evan's dead. There's nothing we can do about that. We got to cover our own asses."

"What about Nose?" I asked.

Snicklesnort: "Nose started all this by smacking you. Don't be sticking out your neck for that boy. There's no future in it."

In the afternoon I was back in the library. Miss Lovitt wanted to talk with me. "Are you okay, Bowser?"

"Yeah, Miss Lovitt, I'm fine. If you don't have anything I need to do right now, may I go outside a minute?"

She looked worried. "Where to?" she asked.

"Just to the stoop." I said.

"Okay, just to the stoop, Bowser. Promise me. This would not be a good time to get into any trouble."

I promised.

I must have been stressed out because I was saying lines to myself like, "The sky is blue and the clouds are high," as though describing things around me was important, as though that would somehow help keep me safe. The air was warm and lazy with insect sounds, and I felt I was hiding out in the open: fair game for anyone. I wanted out, but I couldn't imagine what out looked like.

Miss Lovitt came out on the porch. "Talk to me, Bowser."

"I'm in a tight spot," I said.

She sat down next to me on the edge of the stoop. "Talk to me."

Everything about this seemed dangerous. I felt I was lowering my guard and closing my eyes, wide open for a pummeling, and having her sit next to me and coax me made everything, somehow, more frightening. She wore teacher clothes: loose pants, flower-print cotton shirt; she could have been my mother or a sister or a girlfriend.

I tried to explain to her that everyone was lying about how Evan got killed.

She seemed impatient. "So, Bowser, what are you worried about?"

"Nothing seems real," I said. "It's like Evan never really died and was never really here."

"Is that it? Someone has offended your sense of reality? If that's what you think your problem is, you are definitely in a tight spot. What about Evan?"

"Yeah, it's like he was never here."

"Did you know him? Did you care about him?" She was almost barking.

"He was my locker mate," I said.

"I'm not asking whether you shared cigarettes or cookies. Did you care about him?"

I was getting uncomfortable. "Listen, we weren't queer for each other or anything."

Miss Lovitt slumped forward. "Bowser, I'd like to believe that you can grasp something beyond masturbating. Can you try to be a little less of an ass?"

I wasn't sure I was following her.

"How about Nose?" she asked.

I wanted to shut this down, so I said, "Some of my best friends are niggers."

She looked at her shoes. Then she stood up and walked in through the door.

It was a tough week with no friends, and I took a lot from the other boys. I got to dread time in Cottage

B. At least at school we sat at separate desks and there was a teacher watching. And Miss Lovitt was there in the library, even though we didn't talk much. In the cottage there were too many of us to avoid one another. I retreated into *Heart of Darkness* as best I could. When the boys insulted me, I pretended not to hear. If a boy punched or kicked me, I punched or kicked back and then retreated; I tried not to engage.

Saturday I was back at my office under the tree. Babybird came up. "Professor, I always stood up for you, you know I did. When the other boys would be talking about you always having your head stuck in a book, I told them you was learning more than we was." I had been listening to Evan's radio/cassette player. A tape was still in it, and I got an idea. I grabbed it and pulled it onto my lap. I turned off the radio as though it were distracting me from what Babybird was saying, but at the same time, I pressed RECORD.

Babybird went on. "I want to warn you. Snickle-snort done told the Nub about you. You got to watch your back. You better find some way to tell Shorty Nub that you going to tell the story his way."

"Thanks, Babybird. I want to do that, but I wasn't there. Nobody ever told me the way I'm supposed to tell it."

"First of all, you ain't supposed to say that Shorty Nub wasn't there when the root fell on Evan."

"Was he there?"

"No, he'd went off with Mr. Greenjeans. But if we tell it that way, all of us could get in hot water." Babybird told everything.

When we heard the call to line up, I pressed the STOP button and switched to radio. Babybird jumped when he heard "Cloud Nine" start at the middle. He asked, "Didn't you hear Mr. Lindquist call lineup?"

I lay back and said, "Mr. Lindquist can kiss my ass."

Babybird shook his head and said, "You really are nuts."

I sat there under the tree listening to the radio and waiting to be missed in roll call. I had actual proof in taped testimony from an eyewitness: a bird in the hand, so to speak. Mr. Lindquist would have to see the true story. Then maybe things would start to come right.

I could see that Mr. Lindquist had gotten another housefather to watch his boys, and he was headed up the hill after me.

When he got close and saw me lying back under the tree, he didn't look so much pissed as disgusted. "What are you pulling now, Bowser?" he asked.

"I needed to talk with you alone," I told him.

Mr. Lindquist was showing no interest as he stood above me with his arms crossed. "What did you want to say to me, Bowser?"

"Mr. Lindquist, Nose didn't have anything to do with the accident. It all happened because Shorty Nub left the team alone."

Now Mr. Lindquist looked both disgusted and amazed. "Bowser, you weren't even there! Besides, who said anything about Nose causing the accident? And why would you want to cover for Nose if they did?"

"I know I wasn't there, Mr. Lindquist, but please listen to this tape. Babybird was there, and I got him telling how it happened."

"Give me the tape." I offered it up to him from where I sat on the ground. He shoved it in his pocket and said, "So now you're taping other boys' conversations?"

"Will you listen to it?" I pleaded.

"Maybe you really are nuts," Mr. Lindquist said. "Just get up and fall in, Bowser."

In my bunk, I couldn't sleep. Mr. Lindquist was the same as Mr. Silver and Dr. Garcia. None of them believed me or were even interested enough to listen. This time I was in serious danger. If Mr. Lindquist let any of the boys know that I had taped Babybird, I was dead. As it got closer to dawn, I half dreamed visions of Shorty Nub standing over me with the bat, telling me to take my pants down, and all the boys snickering, spitting on me, waiting their turn to beat me, to violate me. By the time Mr.

Lindquist came in to rouse us, it was all I could do not to scream as we made our beds:

> O Lord my God, in thee do I take refuge;
> save me from all my pursuers, and deliver me,
> lest like a lion they rend me, dragging me away,
> with none to rescue.

Throughout the morning, I panicked every time anyone came close to me. In class, boys were acting up, and Mr. Waters said, "Why don't you all try acting human a little bit, like Bowser here. He never does anything wrong." I looked at the desk, rubbing my hand up and down my leg. I imagined that one of them would see that I was defenseless, and he would yell out to the others, and they would rush at me like lions, and they would tear me apart.

At lunch I force-fed myself a few bites to try to appear a little normal. No one had shown much sign of noticing anything different about me. By the time I got to the library, I felt as if I were pulling up on a lifeboat, even though Miss Lovitt looked at me almost like I shouldn't exist. I sat and stared at the open page of *Heart of Darkness* and thought about the mess I was in, but I forgot to turn the page.

I guess Miss Lovitt noticed that, because she sat next to me and asked, "Bowser, are you all right?"

It took me a while to respond. I was still looking at the page when I said, "No, ma'am. I'm afraid I'm in a jam."

Miss Lovitt said, "Talk to me, Bowser."

I couldn't get myself to speak.

"Okay," she said. "You were not given the opportunity to grieve for Evan. You were offended that no one around you expressed grief and that they wanted to divide his belongings. That's good: You should have been angry. You have a right to grieve. And you believe you know what really happened that day and that people are lying about it. But that doesn't make you any less alive or Evan any less dead or take away that you had cared for him and shared some of your life with him."

I asked, "May I go out to the stoop? I just need to get some fresh air."

"I think I'll join you," she said.

The stoop was in a rectangle of deep shade, but everything beyond was bright and seared, the air beating with insects.

I said, "It's not only that—grieving. I think I'm really in danger. I think someone is going to hurt me bad, maybe even kill me."

Miss Lovitt looked doubtful, and cocked her head a little, as though she wasn't sure if I was being paranoid. "Who do you think is out to get you, Bowser?"

"I told you about Mr. Palmer going off before Evan got killed and about Nose getting pinned for it. I've been trying to tell people the truth, but no one will touch it. The white boys think I'm squealing on them after I got them into this mess. Yesterday it got worse. I taped a boy telling the truth and gave the tape to Mr. Lindquist. He won't touch it either. Now, if any of the boys finds out about it, I'm worse than dead. Plus, the black boys think I'm getting Nose sent down to Lorton and that I'm the leader behind the white boys framing Nose."

Miss Lovitt was still listening. "Will Mr. Lindquist protect you from the other boys?" she asked.

"Mr. Lindquist is disgusted because he thinks I'm an asshole and a little nuts. Plus, there's Shorty Nub. I know it's gotten back to him that I'm saying he walked away and let Evan get killed. I'll be lucky to live long enough to get sent to the asylum. Maybe I'd be better dead."

Miss Lovitt said, "Cut it out, Bowser." She was starting to look worried. "You really are in danger, aren't you? Why have you put yourself in this fix with the boys and Mr. Lindquist and Shorty Nub?"

"I had to tell the story true."

"You weren't even there. Why couldn't you just keep your mouth shut?"

"Because it seemed that all these bullshit stories were making it so nothing was real, and I wasn't real and Evan had never been real and Evan wasn't dead and I wasn't alive."

"So you are risking your body and life to defend

your sense of reality, to prove you are alive? Does that really make any sense to you?" she asked.

I thought about it, and it did make sense to me. I didn't understand why she couldn't see it.

"Bowser," she said, "if that is the only reason you want to get beaten to death, my advice is forget it, change your story and shut up. Correcting stories so that they are literally true is never going to make you or Evan alive or real."

She was hanging her head and thinking hard. Then she looked up at me impatiently. "How about Evan? Does he matter at all? What does the wrong story do to Evan? How about Nose, for God's sake? What does the story do to Nose?"

I was not getting this but tried to go along. "Evan? He's dead."

"What difference does it make if the story about him dying isn't true?"

"Well, it's like using him, using his death. It makes him like a punk."

"What about Nose?

"Nose is on his way to Lorton."

"Does he deserve to go there?"

"No. Nose didn't want to hurt anybody. He just wants to be a store man."

"Do you want to save him?"

"I would if I could."

"Do you believe his story?"

"You know I do."

"Why?"

"I know him. He wouldn't kill Evan."

"You trust Nose?"

My instinct at first told me that this was some sort of trap. I looked at her for a moment, and I said, "Yeah."

"Bowser, maybe I can help you," she said. "I don't know. I'm not sticking my neck out if this is just about your sense of reality."

I thought maybe this lady could actually help me in some way. So I said, "I hang out with him in the boiler room. We collect insects and talk about everything. When I started huffing spot remover, he tried to knock me straight."

"You have to tell me, one time. Why are you doing this?"

"To keep Nose out of Lorton."

"Why?"

"He's my homeboy."

Then she put her arm around my shoulders. The smell of hay drifted up on the breeze from the river. I could not picture myself riding a motorcycle. I pictured myself tied down with my arms pinned behind me.

Miss Lovitt said, "Bowser, if you want to get real, worry about helping Nose. Don't worry so much about the story."

· 10 ·

MAD DOG

BACK IN THE COTTAGE, they didn't call me Bowser or Professor anymore. If they talked to me at all, they called me Mad Dog. I withdrew and read—or pretended to read—and just watched. I watched for any sign that Mr. Lindquist had told them that I had taped Babybird. I watched for Shorty Nub, how he would come after me or who would come after me for him. And I watched the black boys, who seemed to me always circling.

I came to focus on what Miss Lovitt told me: It wasn't enough to get the story straight; what I needed to do was save Nose. But I couldn't see any damn way to do it. The only beginning point I could think of was to position myself. I decided to make myself as strong and clear as I could and not allow myself to space out into story time.

There were some weights that Gray was allowed to take to the area outside the showers. "Let me work out with you," I pleaded. Gray was doing sixty-pound curls. He didn't answer me. He didn't even look at me—as though I were a gnat on his neck that he would swat if he didn't have his hands full.

After his set, I started trying to take the weights off the barbells. He grabbed me by the throat, stood me up, and slammed me in the belly so hard it knocked my breath out. Then he grabbed me again by the throat and stood me up. His sweating face was right in mine, and he said, "I ain't playing." He let me down, and I crawled over to the wall and sat cradling my belly until he was through with his next set.

Between his sets I got up, walked over to the barbells, squatted, and tried to take the weights off again. When Gray kicked me, a bolt of pain shocked up my spine. I fell over sideways at first. Then I stood up and slowly limped back to my table.

Snicklesnort said to everyone at the table, "Mad Dog is itching to get his ass kicked."

Babybird pitched in, "I think he's got rabies."

I carried *Heart of Darkness* with me all the time, but I didn't read it much. Instead, while looking at a page, I would replay Evan's story, looking for a thread to get hold of. I hoped I could find that and pull it, and if I did, the curtain would unravel and I'd be looking at a way to get Nose out of this jam.

I tried seeing the story through the Nub's eyes. He was gone somewhere. He came back and Evan had been killed. If he needed to keep himself covered, there should have been some easy way for him to explain it so he wasn't there at all. He could have said he had to respond to an emergency or go for more water and his radio didn't work.

The most important thing to the Nub was that nobody know he was gone. It was so important that he was willing to go to a lot of trouble to concoct a story that put him on the tractor when it killed Evan. It put him right where the accident happened, but it was just about the perfect alibi to prove that he wasn't somewhere else. Where had he gone, and what had he done there? Snickle had told stories about the Nub leaving the hill and coming back drunk. Was that all?

By breakfast, I'd thought of something. There might still be one person I could trust and who might be willing to touch that glowing coal—the true story—for the sake of Nose: Mr. Woodrow. He might even be able to find out where the Nub was when he left the crew.

Shorty Nub would get Mr. Woodrow to work with Mr. Greenjeans on repairs. Mr. Greenjeans would rib Mr. Woodrow like he was in a minstrel show. Mr. Woodrow would let his white co-worker tease him but would get the better of him. Mr. Greenjeans could tease Mr. Woodrow, but he could not worry him.

Once, I had gone with Mr. Woodrow to help Mr. Greenjeans fix a roof. Greenjeans sent Mr. Woodrow to get something, and when he came back, Greenjeans started on him.

"You a handy man, Mr. Woodrow. Yes, sir. How'd you get so handy? Playing pocket pool?"

Mr. Woodrow's good nature didn't strain a bit. He said, "You look like you a handy man yourself. Why, I bet if your hand was sandpaper and your dick was wood, you wouldn't even have a pecker."

Mr. Woodrow might be able to find out something from Mr. Greenjeans. If not, maybe he could get the story from somebody outside. Woodrow had friends and kin all over Goochland County. The problem was, even if Mr. Woodrow was willing, I couldn't see clearly where finding out this information would lead. Like taping Babybird or trying to tell the straight story to Mr. Silver, getting anyone else to touch it was still going to be hard. Plus, even I wondered if I wasn't a little nuts.

Nuts or not, I had to help my friend this time, and this plan was all I could come up with.

When it came library duty time, I felt that I had to tell Miss Lovitt about my scheme. When I did, she looked worried, but in the end she allowed me to go look for Mr. Woodrow to tell him she needed a lightbulb changed. I found him taking a break in the boiler room. He heard me coming in the door and was looking at me with those big round, smiling eyes of his. You couldn't startle him.

"Mr. Woodrow, Miss Lovitt wants you to change a lightbulb."

"She in a hurry, is she?"

"No, sir."

"She ain't in a hurry, but she sent you to fetch me?"

"Can I sit down and talk to you for a minute?" I asked.

"Sure you can, Bowser dog. What you want to talk about?"

"I just wanted to ask you about Mr. Greenjeans."

"Who?"

"The white guy who always wears overalls that Shorty Nub has you working with on repairs."

"Oh, you talking about Mr. Silvy! What about him, Bowser dog?"

"You know, sometimes when Shorty Nub is running boss on special force, Mr. Silvy comes up in the pickup truck and they disappear."

Mr. Woodrow was still smiling, but he was thinking, too. "I reckon they jest going to get supplies."

"But they don't always come back with supplies. Plus, Shorty Nub comes back smoked up sometimes."

"I wouldn't know nothing about that." He was smiling, but I knew he was shutting down.

I shrugged. "You know anything about Nose?"

"I hear they sending him off to Lorton."

"You know anything about that place, Mr. Woodrow?"

"I did some electrical work down there one time."

"What was it like?"

"It was like animal cages—just concrete and bars and barbed wire. Dark, too. They didn't waste much electricity on light."

"I only know about the boys they send there," I said. "Hardrocks."

"Yeah, all the boys I seen go that way was hard and mean cases."

"What do you think about Nose going that way?"

"Nose ain't no hardrock. He don't want to do nothing but be a store man."

"Yeah, Mr. Woodrow, but I tell you what, if they try putting him in an animal cage, they are going to have an animal on their hands. If we could just show that Shorty Nub left his post the day Evan died, maybe we could blow up this whole story."

Mr. Woodrow looked at me with cold eyes.

Then, just as though we'd been talking about sports, he said, "Good to talk with you, Bowser dog, but I got to get down here and change a lightbulb."

"Just think about it, Mr. Woodrow," I tried, but he acted as though he didn't hear. Even Mr. Woodrow wouldn't touch it.

That night after dinner, I went back to the shower room corner. Gray said, "Get lost, Mad Dog."

I didn't say anything; I just watched him do his first set. When he finished the first set, he said, "I told you to get out of here."

Since I stayed out of team sports, I had gotten in the habit instead of going outside from the library every afternoon to do sit-ups, push-ups, and even some exercises from the yoga book. Now I dropped to the floor and did twenty push-ups. Gray did another set. I did twenty sit-ups. Gray did another set. I did twenty push-ups. By the time he finished working out, I had done one hundred push-ups and one hundred sit-ups.

I guess when they saw me go back there, the guys from my table took bets whether I'd come out in one piece or not.

When I got back to the table, Snickle said, "So, Nose is gone. What are you, Gray's girl now?" He was leaning back on his chair smoking. I grabbed the chair and pulled it hard. Snickle went flying and broke the back of his head against the wall, then smacked it again hitting the floor. I was standing over him, watching to see if he was conscious and thinking about kicking him in the face if he was. Babybird tackled me, and we went tumbling over some chairs. Then Mr. Lindquist came through and broke it up.

After he called Mr. Franklin to take a look at

Snicklesnort's head, Mr. Lindquist asked Snickle what had happened. "I don't know," Snickle whined. "I was leaning back, and the chair came out from under me."

Next afternoon I was out on the stoop thinking through everything—thinking that if Mr. Woodrow wouldn't touch it, I didn't have a plan B—when I saw Mr. Woodrow's hulk far away by the barn. He was moving side to side like a bear as he walked. I watched him walk slowly across the field until I could see that he was coming to me. When he got to the stoop, he nodded and sat down.

"Hot one, ain't it?" he said.

"Hot enough for me," I said.

"Bowser dog, if you was to get some goods on Shorty Nub, what would you do with that?"

"I would tell it to Miss Lovitt and let her tell the bosses."

"She couldn't prove nothing without telling who told her. That could put you and me in a hot place."

I chewed a stem of grass and turned this over. "How bad is what he's doing?"

"Can't say for sure yet."

"Moonshine?"

"Maybe. I expect a whole lot worse, too."

"How about this? Miss Lovitt's boyfriend is a cop. Somebody tells me when Shorty Nub is going to do something again. By then, if we can't think of any better way to blow the whistle, we could tip off Miss Lovitt and ask her to pass the word to her friend."

Mr. Woodrow smiled and said, "Hot as hell out here, ain't it?"

"It's hot all right. What do you think of my plan?"

"Not much. The more people involved, the riskier it gets for everybody. I know Miss Lovitt's beau, Cal Sasser, but I don't know him that good. If we can't think of nothing better, though, I reckon your plan's better than nothing."

"What is the Nub up to?"

———

I ain't never messed in nobody's bidness before, but it'd break my heart to see Nose get sent down without me even trying to do nothing about it. I reckon I'm going to step in it this time.

I don't know much about what the Nub and Silvy is up to, but I know where they doing it. There's an old cinder block deer camp up on the James. My cousin come over last night smoked up good. He started calling that old place the "poon hall." He talked so sloppy I couldn't figure out what all he was talking about. When I started to ask him questions, he got suspicious and said it was a secret, and he wasn't going to tell nobody about it unless they was in the "Poon Hall Hunt Club."

I used to hunt down that way, but then Mr. Palmer

bought it and he don't hunt. He put no-trespassing signs and no-hunting signs all over that place. It's years Mr. Palmer and Mr. Silvy been throwing moonshine parties in a cabin down there. Maybe they got themselves a new bidness. For the past couple years, Mr. Silvy's wife been doing cleaning work down at Barnet School for Girls. Sometimes she gets a crew of little girls to hep her. I don't know nothing for sure, but I got a bad feeling about what happens to some of them girls.

I knew that Mr. Woodrow was a cautious man in his way and that he knew more than he was saying. If he had a bad feeling about the girls, it was because of something his cousin told him that he didn't want to repeat. As I tried to picture the meaning of Mr. Woodrow's words, I remembered girls from the Diagnostic Center. Then my mind focused on Audrey Stockton. We used to walk to school together along the railroad tracks, and she'd tell me about running away and getting drunk. She was a little girl, with strawberry hair and pale blue eyes, and I thought she would have been innocent except somehow she couldn't afford to be. For all I knew, Audrey was still at the Barnet School.

"Where's the cabin, Mr. Woodrow?"

"They call it a cabin; it's just a bunkhouse made of cinder blocks. It's on the left bank of the river, at the third landing upstream from here, where 651 goes closest to the river. Now, I know white and colored trash both, sometimes Indians, too, been going down there to party with hooch and whores."

"Mr. Woodrow, I swear I will not ever tell who told me this, and I will do anything for you for the rest of my life, if you just find out and tell me when they are going to do it again."

Mr. Woodrow lay back smiling. "Bowser dog, I want you to tell me two things. First, does Miss Lovitt know you talking to me? Second, why is it you going to all this trouble?"

"Sir," I said, "I told Miss Lovitt that I was going to ask you for your help, but she doesn't need to know anything more. I'm doing this because Nose is my homeboy, and I don't want to see him get sent down. Will you get the time for me? And please, Mr. Woodrow, please don't take them on yourself without telling me. If something went wrong, I could be stuck forever without ever knowing the true story. And you know the Nub would come after me."

"Well, Bowser dog, I reckon they laying low since Evan got killed. But once it quiet down and they feel safe, I reckon they be at it again. Best thing you can do is hep put Shorty Nub's mind at ease so he relax and go back to it."

After that I knew I had to face Shorty Nub. When we started lining up for dinner, I broke line and walked right up to Snicklesnort and punched him. The rest you could predict. Mr. Lindquist broke it up, and I got put on force.

Mr. Lindquist had covered for me the last time. He kept me off force before he knew I'd been huffing Carbona. He sure as hell wouldn't do it again. Starting the fight in the dining hall made it so he couldn't cover for me this time even if he wanted to.

Next morning when I fell out of line, Shorty Nub told me to ride in the cab.

"I ain't seen you since the first two weeks when they brought you up, but I heard that you out of your mind. Reading books all the time, ain't you?"

"I like to read," I said.

"What do you like to read?"

"Literature mostly. History."

"Personally, I think that's a lot of nonsense. I don't think that's what you need. I think you need some common sense."

"What do you mean?"

"I mean, you ain't got the sense to stay out of trouble. You in a mess of trouble right now and you don't even know it."

"Sir, I think you got me all wrong. Evan was my locker mate, so I was rattled when he died. I guess I kind of got confused too, because I was in lockdown with Nose and he fed me a story about the whole thing. I'm straight now. I mean, I wasn't even there, but all of my cottage boys have told me that Nose was just trying to pin it on everybody else to cover his own ass. Nose always had it in for me. I hope the bastard rots in Lorton."

"So why you mixing it up with Side? I thought he was supposed to be your homeboy?"

"He was my homeboy, but then he started calling me a punk."

"You poor boy. He hurt your feelings?"

"He keeps calling me a punk and I'm going to hurt more than his feelings."

We got to the barn where we were to throw up hay bales, and Snicklesnort was bristling, tight-lipped. He wanted a chance to get at me. Shorty Nub told everyone where to throw the bales and called me and Snickle apart to go around behind the barn.

"I think you two boys ought to have a meeting of the minds," said Shorty Nub.

Snicklesnort said, "I ain't going to stand for him pulling my chair out from under me and sucker punching me."

I said, "I ain't going to stand for you calling me a punk."

"Why don't you boys settle it right here? I'll give you two minutes." Snicklesnort squared off, squatting down with both hands open. He led with a left and grabbed my shirt with his right to try to pull me to come up in my face with his knee. He left himself wide open for a right, and I nailed him on the jaw. I could have followed with a combination, but I didn't. I blocked and weaved as he came in punching, but I did not counterpunch. After a little dancing around and jabbing, he lit into me with a barrage and caught me on the right of my head, hard, then followed to my belly, and I bent over. He would have come up into my face with his knee, but Shorty Nub stepped in and stopped him.

"Okay," Shorty Nub said, "now y'all boys are even. I want you to shake hands and get this behind you."

Snicklesnort was out of breath but pleased with himself. "You mess with me again and I'll tear you up."

I said, "You quit calling me a punk, and I'll quit messing with you."

Shorty Nub yelled, "SHAKE!" and we did.

The Nub told Snicklesnort to go back in the barn. When we were alone, the Nub said to me, "There now. You get back with your own boys, and everything will work out. I don't know what kind of game you playing with the shrinks, and I don't care. If you want to get sent to a hospital, go on. But just don't you cross me."

I said, smiling, "Well, sir, I am unstable, if you know what I mean. Maybe you could help get me the treatment I need."

Shorty Nub laughed out loud and shook his head. "You are a nut," he said.

· 11 ·

SHOOT THE HUMP

THE REST OF THE WEEK on special force I kept up the lovable nut act, joking and good natured with Shorty Nub. I played that I was trying to seek drag with the Nub so he would help me get off the Hill for treatment. I kept my focus on doing what I could to let him relax and not see me as a threat. Maybe if he got comfortable with the idea that I wasn't going to cause any trouble for him and that Nose wouldn't be able to, he'd go back to his old ways so that Mr. Woodrow could set him up.

The fight put things back on beam with Snickle-snort, and working together helped, too. I followed his lead in the field and made him laugh whenever I could. Snicklesnort was my homeboy, always had been. I liked his stories, and I tried not to let his drag with Shorty Nub get in the way.

Shorty Nub was a different story. Every time I did the horsing around with him it made me sick to my stomach. I would think of Audrey Stockton— pretty and chain-smoking along the train tracks or alone with me on the rocks in the woods—and I imagined her taken to this rundown shack in the country by the likes of Shorty Nub and Mr. Green-jeans and their toothless trash buddies. I couldn't stop images drifting up of what the place would actually look like and smell like: an animal pen with the stench of decay.

Kissing up to Shorty Nub made me feel like I was part of his hell. To live with it, I started dreaming stories of how I would get him and building on them every night. My favorite was garroting the Nub in the courtyard. It went like this: I carry in my pocket everywhere the garrote Ben Susan had given me. While I wait for the bust, I work out every day and build up my strength. Then the day comes when Miss Lovitt tells me that they busted the party, but Shorty Nub doesn't know it yet. At lineup for dinner, I fall out formally, step to face Shorty Nub as though I had been called. I stand to attention and smile in his face. Then suddenly, precisely, mechanically, I step behind him and I wrap the garrote around his throat and pull it tight. His eyes bulge, and I whisper in his ear, "This is for Audrey and for Nose and for Evan." I would recite this line mentally and edit the scene like a film. I pull the garrote with a thousand pounds of force; I feel it cut through the spinal cord, and I see his head fall to the ground. I am covered with blood that cleanses, purifies, sanctifies.

One part of the story I lived out every day was the exercise. At first I hung out with Gray doing push-ups and sit-ups while he worked weights. The only reason Gray had been so hard on me was to stand up for Nose. He still thought I was trying to get Nose sent down. I trusted him because he was loyal to Nose and he was trying to get his back.

Finally I told him about how I wanted to save Nose from going down and how I hadn't figured out how to do it yet but that I wanted to be in shape. He must have believed me after he'd thought about it because he started letting me work out on the weights. I matched him set for set with lower weights, pushing to get as strong as he was. Every time I worked out, I thought of myself as in training to slay Shorty Nub. There was still story time and there was still Hill time. Now, though, I had a story time that was private, and my private stories did not drift. I cultivated them; I exercised them.

After getting right with Snicklesnort, everything fell back into place at my table. Boys started calling me Bowser again, and we went back to putting together wild stories at the table. Mr. Lindquist even started treating me with a little less disgust. As time passed, my fear of Mr. Lindquist letting other boys know I had recorded Babybird also began to fade. Something else was going on for me now. I fell to waiting, sharpening myself like a knife, and waiting.

After I got off force, I started going back to the library in the afternoons. Miss Lovitt couldn't help but ask, "Bowser, did you have a chance to talk with Mr. Woodrow?"

"No, ma'am." I looked at her with a stone blank face, so that she could see that I couldn't talk. I knew that Mr. Woodrow's life might depend on how well I could keep it a secret that he was out to get the goods on the Nub.

"If I can help in any way, or if I can get Cal to help, will you let me know?"

"Yes, ma'am, I will."

It was very hard for her to let it go, but she did.

The plan to send me to a hospital was still cooking, but I didn't think about it as much. One day Mr. Lindquist called me aside and said, "They're making arrangements for you to transfer to the hospital at the end of the month. I hope you know what the hell you are doing."

"I do," I said. The fights with Snicklesnort probably helped my case. Shorty Nub might have helped too. It would only be to his advantage that I was certified loony, in case I wanted to tell any stories he didn't like.

I sat on the stoop every afternoon and watched the barn across the field, hoping up the form of Mr. Woodrow's big frame slowly moving toward me.

After dinner one evening, Snickle was leaning into a story again. "Old Shorty Nub is back to his old ways. Mr. Greenjeans came and they went off for supplies, only this time he left us digging drainage ditches in the shade." I couldn't believe I was hearing this.

"He left you alone with the crew?" I asked.

Snickle replied, "Yeah, he had a long talk with me first about how he needed to trust me and I needed to be worthy of that trust. Same old shit."

Mr. Woodrow had not told me anything about this. Who knew what might be happening to those girls. And Nose could get sent down any day. When I tried to get my bearings, I couldn't see a next step.

By morning the plan was gone. I was no longer waiting for anything but to get close enough to Shorty Nub to get a wire around his throat. It might not do Nose any good, but it wouldn't do any harm. Maybe it would get people interested enough to ask more questions, and the Nub wouldn't be there to keep the boys straight on the alibi. Anyway, I was going to kill the man. I had to.

I figured I would have to bide my time a little longer. If I tried to rush him, the other staff would have me before I could get to him. I didn't think I

could risk doing something obvious to get on special force. It was too soon after last time; they were likely to lock me down instead.

Next day at meals, I watched Shorty Nub and I felt the wire in my pocket, and I waited for him to get close enough, but he did not. That night I saw the whole thing again: I would wait like a panther, and when he came close, I would step out precisely, deliberately. I would stand before him. Then, in an instant, I would be behind him with the garrote around his throat. In another instant, his head would be severed. Then the blood would gush like water from a fountain.

At breakfast next morning, Shorty Nub was coming down the line, staring the boys down and stopping occasionally to ask a question or crack a joke. "I hear you laying them like greased lightning over at the brick shop, Campbell. When you get out, why don't you come over my place and build me a barbecue?" As he came down the line, my heart was shaking my body. I looked straight ahead and had to concentrate on each breath to keep from panting. I felt I was acting in story time; I was dreaming the Nub toward me. My hands were in my back pockets, the wire in the fingers of my right hand. When he was just ten arm-lengths away, my whole body drew back, but when he stopped in front of Snicklesnort, I made my legs step out. All drawing back was over.

The feel of the wire in my fingers aimed me like a rifle.

He got close enough for me to lunge at him and get the wire around his throat. I was still waiting for him to come two more steps to a trigger point when I heard Mr. Woodrow's deep voice across the dining hall yell, "Mr. Palmer, Mr. Palmer, come here quick!"

The Nub said to me, "Get back in line, you nut, this ain't no hospital," and he strode away toward Mr. Woodrow.

I played the scene back like a movie, to convince myself that I had not faltered. By the time I got my tray of food, I knew that I would have done it, that I would do it. This was good; it was a dry run at no cost. Confidence washed through me now, as blood would wash me clean.

I felt all morning that I was free. I knew what I would do, and I knew they would take me away. I was sure of the worst, so there was nothing to be afraid of.

It was raining when I went over to the library in the afternoon, and fluorescent lights buzzed and flickered strangely against the dark gray out the window. Doom lay over the Hill, smug.

I was floating there, in that doom comfort, when Mr. Woodrow stuck his head in the room. He bowed his head to Miss Lovitt. "Miss, I do hate to trouble you, but could I get Bowser dog here to hep me with a busted drain spout? That is, if he ain't hepping you."

Miss Lovitt was alert, and I was afraid she'd blurt out something she shouldn't, but she kept her cool. "Go with Mr. Woodrow, Bowser," she said, "and try not to track mud back in." I put on my yellow hooded raincoat and followed Mr. Woodrow.

As soon as we were down the hall I asked him, "Shorty Nub left the Hill two days ago. Why didn't you tell me?"

He hushed me with his big hand. "Listen to me before you say anything," he said. "I got the whole picture pretty good now." Outside in the rain he said, "You know the suspicion I had about Mrs. Silvy and the girls from over at the Barnet School? Well, it turns out that she gets some of them little girls involved in drugs and invites them away to party. Sometimes she'll take one of them away alone, and that little girl ends up drugged asleep and taken away by Mr. Silvy in the back of a truck to Mr. Palmer's hunt shack. At the shack, Palmer and Silvy and their customers do what they want with her. Then, before Mrs. Silvy takes that girl back to the school, Mrs. Silvy tells her that if she tells a soul they'll see she's dead before anyone believes her. The other day, they was just getting ready for the next party. It's going to be tomorrow."

At first the news hit me hard, and it took time to

recoil from disgust and pity. Only then did it occur to me that I wouldn't kill Shorty Nub with my own hands. The rain was coming down hard and felt good on my face. But when I started to think about what would come next, I knew I couldn't just stay put and wait for news. I had primed myself to kill Shorty Nub; I'd already lit the fuse, and I couldn't unlight it. I had to act.

"Thank you, Mr. Woodrow," I said finally. "I've got to go to the restroom, but I'll be right back" He looked at me funny and nodded.

I would not wait this time. I could not wait for Mr. Woodrow nor Miss Lovitt nor anyone else. I was going to have in my hands the hard evidence. Direct, physical evidence, corpus delicti. And Nose would not go down.

I headed right back into the library as if there were an emergency. "Miss Lovitt, Mr. Woodrow asked me to get you right away."

"What for?"

"I think he's sick. Come quick."

She grabbed her raincoat and ran out. I ran to the bookshelf where the atlases were and grabbed the book of Virginia maps. Then I ran to her desk and pulled out the drawer where she kept her purse and grabbed it. Miss Lovitt was yelling after me as I sprinted down the hall, groping for her car keys in the bag. Then I was out again in the pouring rain.

Lightning flashed and I saw her white Camaro. Then I was in the dry car and tried to ease it down the drive so I wouldn't arouse suspicion. You could hardly see out the windshield; no one could see in either. Bradley Davis had taught me to drive and had let me drive his car. Driving was one thing I was good at.

I drove down the road behind the dining hall, down the hill past the Intake Cottage, and then I could see the gate ahead under a streetlamp in the gray and rain. I drove smoothly up to about twenty feet short of the gate. Then I floored her and busted through just like in a movie.

The gate guard started to walk up to the car before I accelerated, then jumped back and fell on his ass, and his radio went flying. It wouldn't be long before he would raise an alarm and they'd call out the men and dogs. I figured they'd start the dogs wherever they found the car, so I gunned her west on 522 away from the river about a mile and then ran her over a field until she got stuck in a swale. It might take them a little while to find it back there.

I was trembling as I pulled the billfold out of Miss Lovitt's purse and fumbled for the map book. I closed the door behind me and started to backtrack toward the river. It was difficult not to run. In ten minutes or so I made it to the cover of woods. In another half hour I was at the riverbank.

If it wasn't for the heavy rain, I don't think I could have made it without someone seeing me, but I could see that the river was already beginning to rise. The soggy map book shook in my hands as I confirmed the location of the deer camp according to what Mr. Woodrow described: upstream, left bank, third landing, where 651 comes closest to the river. I counted the bends upriver to where the landing should be.

I remember thinking as I stepped into the water that I'd sooner drown than be caught and that drowning was more likely. My first steps were toward midriver until I reached a big channel. I threw the map book in the water there and made sure it got a good floating start, then did the same with my raincoat. The channel was wide enough in the middle and the current strong enough that, if I was lucky, these clues would come to shore miles downstream and lure men and dogs in that direction.

It was not going to be easy heading upstream. The best way to attempt it would be to grasp the bank with my hands while walking the edge of the river, if it weren't for the dogs. I couldn't leave any scent along the bank. I stayed out far enough that I wouldn't touch the bank if I fell, and I inched up, taking baby steps, stumbling, falling in the water every few feet, until I was under the bridge. Then I swam and crawled, holding my whole body and most of my head under water, until I reached the middle pilings. There was a buildup of logs around them, and I was able to fashion a quick tent of leaves and twigs so that I could breathe in it and not be seen until nightfall.

I was most afraid of a flash flood, but it had been a long dry summer, so the water had still not risen to its high mark on the banks. After dark I could see lights moving in the woods way downstream and the reflection of headlights from the bridge in the choppy water all around me. I crept upstream and toward the bank I'd come from, right into Belmont.

I was less worried about the hounds right in the facility, so I waded up along the bank, holding on to roots and branches. I waded all night upriver against a rising current that was like darkness rushing through darkness through the hush of rain. Now and then lightning flashed with a crack of thunder close on it. I fell often, and I was bruised and cut all over my shins, arms, and palms. Over and over, I stepped in over my head; over and over, I got to the point where I fell in the water and didn't want to get up. My pants and my brogues were heavy, and my muscles had given out, and had given out again.

The whole night I struggled against the current, was forced back, fell against rocks, gave up, and then pulled myself up again because I had no choice but to make my body go on. At times I felt like I was only making it forward by the inch.

Finally, long numb and shivering, I reached the landing as the sky began to glow dull behind me like a flashlight through gauze. I pulled my limp legs onto the bank and walked a few yards before I saw the cinder block houses of the old deer camp and a camper trailer off to the left. Then I pulled back into the woods along the bank, sat on a fallen trunk, and watched the gray lighten over the shacks.

I was still numb and spent when I heard something move through the bushes and saw the white head of a dog poke through. He was an English setter, a bird dog, I figured, not a man-hunter. He stopped for a pet, and I looked at a tag around his collar that said, MY NAME IS DUNBAR. He looked like the dog in the painting in the office of the Intake Cottage as he took off across the clearing. I lay back limp with my head against the fallen tree, trying to figure out what to do next. My mind wandered for a minute, and I wondered what that sour smell was. You always smell it in the weeds on a riverbank in the summer. Burdock? Pokeweed?

A motor droned over the river, a fisherman probably. But I was awake enough to startle when I realized it was getting close and heading in toward this landing. I turned to look through the leaves of the bank and saw it was a black man in a johnboat. I thought it was a dream swimming in my tiredness at first, but soon I saw him standing upright in his boat right in front of me: Mr. Woodrow! If I hadn't been close to dead spent, I wouldn't have been able to stop myself from shouting with joy and surprise. I was so excited, I didn't even wonder how he came to be here. He was like a vision of salvation, and it revived me so that I got an inspiration of how to greet him.

Mr. Woodrow cut his motor and slipped to the bank upstream of the landing. He was securing the boat under some overhanging branches when I crept up behind him. When I was about five feet from him in the bushes, I yelled out, "Ain't you done your *reconnoitering*?"

Mr. Woodrow turned and jumped at the same time and fell flat back into the water. I was laughing so hard that we might have lost the boat if I hadn't leaped for the painter at the last minute.

We were both in the water, as though we were being baptized. Mr. Woodrow jumped up and looked at first like he would grab me by the scruff of my neck and drown me like a puppy. Then that big old smile of his spread to bigger than I'd ever seen it, and I think for the first time in his life he couldn't think of a word to say. Finally, he gave me a bear hug, right there in the river, and I felt like a little kid.

He got some Pall Malls out of a tackle box, and we figured it was okay to have a smoke. It was only six o'clock. Nobody would be coming along for a while.

"Mr. Woodrow," I asked, "did anybody call the cops?"

"They surely called them about you running."

"No," I said, "I mean about the Nub's operation."

"Not as I know. I surely didn't. You know I don't like getting involved with the police."

"Then what the hell are you doing here?" I asked.

"Well, Bowser, I didn't have no doubt of where you was headed, and I just didn't want you to be here by yourself."

The nearest cabin was the biggest of the three and looked like it was in the best repair. It had one window with an air conditioner and boards above that. The only way you could see in was through the door if it were open. There were no windows but the one with the air conditioner.

"Do you reckon they'll come even with the alarm out for me?" I asked him.

Mr. Woodrow thought that over and said, "Nub'd gone yesterday afternoon before you shot the hump, but they'd've called him in to run the hounds last night. On the other hand, he done made arrangements, and he a bold man.

"Bowser, you look out for me. I'm going to go in and inspect that place."

"I wouldn't do that if I were you," I said.

"Oh, you wouldn't?" he said.

"No, sir. If the search men come and I'm standing watch, I couldn't come out and divert them. If it was the Nub or Greenjeans and them, I couldn't either."

"Well," said Mr. Woodrow, "there's something to that."

He pulled a crowbar out of the boat and gave it to me in case I needed it to pry the door. Then he walked to a high place in the woods where he could see a car coming but not far in advance.

The door was solid and bolt-locked, probably reinforced. I clawed at it and banged it and tried every way I could before giving up on getting in that way. I had to work hard and long at the air conditioner to pry it loose and push it in. It was bolted fast. Finally I worked it loose. It crashed to the floor inside and gave me just enough room to crawl in. The generator wasn't turned on, so it was dark. The only light streamed through the rectangle where the air conditioner had been.

The place was about the size of a double-wide trailer. As I felt along the wall, I noticed it turned from rough cinder block to a kind of plush velvet. Then I tripped and found I was on an enormous bed. When I kneeled and tried to crawl off, a metal stand crashed and I heard a big bulb burst. The place itself now seemed haunted with abominations of the flesh. Feeling around with my stomach turning, my fingers found the handle of a filing cabinet. I opened a drawer, and the contents clattered, aluminum against aluminum. Film canisters.

I grabbed one of the canisters and shoved it down my shirt, then opened the next drawer and rummaged with my fingers through folders and found in them the glossy feel of eight-by-ten photos. I grabbed a handful of these and lurched toward the rectangle of light. Holding my shirt closed over the canister, I raised a handful of photos up to the light and saw clearly the photo on top. Abomination. Unnatural abomination of flesh, cruelty, humiliation, pain.

Voices:

MR. WOODROW: "I was just hiking up here to see if he hadn't run upstream a-ways."

SHORTY NUB: "Is that right now? When did handy-man niggers start leading search parties?"

MR. WOODROW: "Well, I was off today, and I thought if I could find him myself, I might could keep him from being hurt."

SHORTY NUB: "Oh, he's going to get hurt, all right."

MR. WOODROW: "I guess he got it coming, after all. I hope you boys find him. I got to be getting back to my truck. Would you all carry me back up there?"

MR. GREENJEANS: "I didn't see no truck."

MR. WOODROW: "I hid her way up yonder, off the road, so Bowser couldn't spot it, and I hiked in."

SHORTY NUB: "Silvy, whyn't we take Mr. Woodrow here to find his truck. Woodrow, I'm going to keep this twelve-gauge aimed right at your gut, you hear? You move without me telling you and I'll cut you in half. Silvy, does our princess need some more medicine to keep her sleeping?"

GREENJEANS: "I don't know what you're talking about."

SHORTY NUB: "It's okay, Roy. I don't expect Mr. Woodrow is going to be telling anyone about anything."

GREENJEANS: "I give her a shot about an hour back. I reckon that'll do her for a right good spell."

SHORTY NUB: "Well, make sure that trailer's locked up good, anyhow."

Crouching in the dark cabin, I knew Mr. Woodrow was drawing them away from me. I couldn't think of a thing to do to save him. I wrapped my arms around my knees and buried my head there. As soon as I heard the truck pull off down the road, I scrambled out the window and ran for cover. Through the leaves, I could see the camper trailer parked up on the drive.

I stowed the pictures and the film in Mr. Woodrow's boat, then I made my legs run back to grab the crowbar and to the camper trailer. The lock on the trailer was stronger than it looked, and before I could force it, tires were crunching closer on the gravel in the distance. My left knee started jerking up and down like the needle of a sewing machine, and I nearly crumbled.

> *O Lord my God, in thee do I take refuge;*
> *save me from all my pursuers, and deliver me,*
> *lest like a lion they rend me, dragging me away,*
> *with none to rescue.*

The girl was blond, an angel in white bell-bottoms and a pink top, sound asleep. I couldn't rouse her. I imagined that when she turned her face it would be Audrey Stockton's as posing for her picture in the yearbook. But when she did wake a little and turn her head, it was another girl with pale delicate features and finely etched eyebrows and freckles.

She didn't weigh much more than a hundred pounds, but a limp body is awkward to carry. I had just gotten across the clearing, moving slowly through the mud with the girl over my shoulder in a fireman's carry, when a white van rounded the corner of woods and entered the clearing. I didn't recognize the van. It must have been the sons of bitches who were supposed to join Shorty Nub's party.

I stowed the girl as gently and quietly as I could in the bow of the boat with her head on an orange life preserver and untied the painters. When I pulled the starter rope the first time and the motor didn't catch, I thought my heart would burst like a potato in a fire.

But the second try worked. As we headed out toward the channel, I could see three men: one in hunting camo with a rifle and two men in bright shirts. The motor took them by surprise, and it seemed they didn't know whether to run after us or away from us. As they turned, I could see their faces, but I'd never seen them before. I guessed Mr. Woodrow was still off with Shorty Nub and Greenjeans, diverting them somehow.

Maybe the man in camo figured out who I was from my uniform. He leveled his rifle and took careful aim through the scope. I was in the channel by then and twisted up to full throttle downstream. The man had time to get off a single shot in front of our bow that skimmed the water beyond us on the port side. I was scared of getting shot and just as scared we would hit something submerged at full throttle, but we were lucky.

The river was up, coffee-colored and frothing around rocks, but not flood stage. Clouds were beginning to clear and a cool haze was rising off the river, with a slight headwind breezing upriver. My whole body ached like one big muscle, and things were blurring together in my eyes. But I was turning the throttle gently and watchful, with a careful hand on the tiller for branches and rocks. Having gone to this much trouble, I was not willing to dump now.

The girl moaned up in the bow and seemed to be

trying to say something, but it was all drug slurred. I pulled up to shore in a little cove that was covered from view by the wet summer leaves of sassafras. I sat on the forward bench and lifted her strawberry head onto my lap. She was so pretty it could break my heart, especially to think that I was protecting her and couldn't let anything harm her. I stroked her hair and asked, "What's your name?"

Her eyes were still mostly closed, and she was working her mouth a little. Then she opened her eyes a little farther and had a troubled look on her face. She covered her eyes with her forearm and said, "P . . . P."

"Your name?" I asked. "Take your time."

"Got to p-pee." she said and started to writhe.

I let us drift down to a little sand spit, jumped out in the shallow water, and pulled the boat up. The girl tried to stand on her own. I took her arm and helped her ashore. As she undid her belt and fly, I couldn't help but feel an ache in my loins, but I felt horrible about it, knowing what she'd just been through, and I forced myself to turn away. It sounded like she was going to pee an ocean. When she was finally through and had buckled her belt, I looked around at her.

She seemed confused, but there was something tough about her. She looked around and then looked dazedly at me, still not ready to speak.

"I don't know what you last remember," I said, "but you were kidnapped by some bad people. I was able to get you free. Now we're headed to where we can get help."

As I watched her there, quiet and mixed up, I wished for a moment that I had another plan: to take her away with me and be free and maybe fall in love. But I knew that was just lunatic kid's stuff, story time. I knew what I had to do, and tired as I was, I still had to do something to try to save Mr. Woodrow and Nose.

I got her back in the johnboat. She had awakened enough to put her head up on the prow with the life jacket for a pillow—still too drugged, I think, to understand completely where she was or what was happening.

A white kingfisher dove through the mist and through the rushing sound of distant rapids, bringing everything out, as a detail in a painting can pull out all the shapes and colors. I imagined our boat through the eyes of a boy come early to fish from the shore, disturbed by the lapping of our wake against the bank: a silver vessel tracking through gray mist with golden hair spilling over the prow.

And I saw myself as I might look to her, coming awake in the bow and looking upstream toward the west: a dirty, bloody boy leaning sternward with the tiller in his hand, clothes blowing back like flags made of grocery bags.

We were through the calm water before long. I had to lift the motor so the prop wouldn't tip us on a rock. I helped the girl take her head off the prow and laid it gently on the deck. Then I arranged her body there so her weight would be stable before we hit the white water. "Where are we?" she asked sleepily.

"Not now," I said. "You just rest, and I'll explain it all to you once we get down the river." I had to try to paddle the boat like a canoe, but it was a sight harder to handle than a canoe. The best I could do was try to keep her from going broadside downstream. On one set of ledges we did get swept sideways and were even headed backward for a spell, but I got her bow forward before we hit some small shelves and falls.

By the time I pulled onto the landing at Belmont, the girl was awake but groggy. I guess a large party was still out after me, so the staff was thin on the ground. I asked her name. Becka. I told her to take her time and walk up to the Intake Cottage, that she was going to be okay and that we were going to get her a doctor and make her comfortable.

"What happened?" she asked. Already she didn't remember what I'd told her about the kidnapping.

"You were kidnapped by some bad people. I got you free, and you're going to be just fine now." Then she looked in my eyes. I saw tears in hers and took her hand. Then I held her for a moment and she let me. She put her head on my shoulder, and we just stood there for a few moments. I wished we were somewhere else, and we could just stay like that for a while.

I forced my legs into a trot up the hill ahead of her, then leaned into a run when the ground leveled, all the way to the Intake Cottage. When the receptionist there saw me, I swear she feared for her life. She was on her radio calling for help.

"I've got to see Mr. Ball," I gasped. "NOW!" Mr. Ball came through the door behind me, and I turned and started sputtering, "Shorty Nub took Mr. Woodrow at gunpoint."

Mr. Ball, looking confused, took a step toward me, as if he would restrain me. "I don't know what you're talking about."

I was yelling and arguing and resisting Mr. Ball's hands on me until Becka stepped in, looked at me, and sank to the floor.

· 12 ·

#00 BUCK

Staff was coming in as I tried to get Mr. Ball to listen to me. He would not call the police. "We need to take care of you and this girl first. Once we know you are okay, there will be time to tell your story."

Before Mr. Ball could stop me, I yelled to every-body in the room, "Somebody call the police! There's kidnap going on at the deer camp where 651 goes to the river. They got Mr. Woodrow and may kill him!"

EMTs took Becka away on a stretcher. Other EMTs checked me over. They took me to the infirmary and dressed my wounds. A sheriff's deputy came in with Mr. Ball. The deputy was trying to interview me, and Mr. Ball was trying to get him to stop to let me rest. I ignored them both and just kept shouting over them that Mr. Woodrow had been kidnapped from the hunting cabin up on the river and exactly where that was.

After they left, I just sat there with an EMT and worried about Mr. Woodrow for what seemed like a couple hours.

Finally Mr. Franklin came in. "The sheriff's deputy talked with the girl, and they finally made enough sense of her story to go take a look. We haven't heard anything more yet. It sounds like that girl is mighty lucky you found her."

He let me shower and brought me a steak dinner. Then they let me lie on a cot, with the fans turning slowly, high above me. They gave me a shot, and I could hear the bricks moan.

I don't know how long I slept, but I woke up in lockdown, aching. After I awakened enough to know I wasn't dreaming, I started to take stock, and I realized that I had saved a girl. And I was going to save Nose. Hard, physical evidence, corpus delicti. I'd stowed it in the bait well of Mr. Woodrow's boat. Then I remembered Mr. Woodrow and that they may have shot him. I prayed for him and Nose the best I could. It might have been the first time I prayed for anybody.

> *Dear Lord, please protect Mr. Woodrow from being shot. He's a good man and always does the best he can. Protect Nose from Lorton, dear Lord. He just wants to do Your will by being a store man and helping the poor. And,*

Lord, protect me from any more strikes against
me. If Nose and Mr. Woodrow join the other
friends I let go down, I don't think I could bear
it. Amen.

Someone rattled the door next to mine, and Nose yelled, "They got you, Bowser? Steady, you hear, homeboy?"

How could Nose still be locked down? It seemed like years. After counting days backward, I realized it had been fewer than thirty days since Evan was killed. I lay on the floor and kicked the door once with both feet. "We're going to get out of here!"

Connor was happy to see me when he brought breakfast: full portions of eggs and bacon and grits, with coffee and juice. "I thought you might like to look at this," he said, handing me the Sunday *Richmond News Leader*.

Right on the front page was a picture of Shorty Nub with his head bowed, in handcuffs, being led from a car to the county courthouse. Next to it was a picture of a burned-out block building in a field, with a caption that read, "Powhatan County: scene of child prostitution and pornography arrest."

I could hardly move on to the article, the photo was so sweet. I was stuck there and studied every lovely detail: the looks of satisfaction on the cops holding his arms, the curve of his arms going behind his back. . . . And I added details that weren't there: that the cuffs were too tight and pinched, that the cops taunted and humiliated him in the car as they rode. . . .

Finally, I tore myself away from the picture to the story, but even as I read, I couldn't help but look back at that photograph. The article started off something like this:

CHILD PORNOGRAPHY RING
ARRESTED IN POWHATAN

Three suspects were arrested when Powhatan County sheriff's deputies closed in on a child prostitution ring. According to authorities, the ring kidnapped girls from the Barnet School for Girls, where one of the suspects was employed, drugged the girls, and forced them into acts of prostitution and pornography.

A 14-year-old girl was rescued from the scene and taken to Medical College of Virginia for observation. A sheriff's spokesperson said the girl had been kidnapped and drugged, but did not appear otherwise harmed at the time of her rescue. Authorities are withholding her identity.

Mr. Frederick Palmer of Powhatan and Mr.
Roy Silvy of Goochland were arrested in a
wooded area along the James River near Belmont School for Boys. Both men were employ-
ees at the Belmont facility. Mr. Silvy's wife,
Beverly Silvy, was arrested later at her home.
Mrs. Silvy is an employee of the Barnet School
for Girls.

Sheriff's deputies closed in on the crime
scene in the woods off Route 651 near the James
River at about 10:00 yesterday morning. Mr.
Silvy was injured resisting arrest. A building at
the scene of the crime had been set ablaze,
deputies said, before authorities arrived at the
scene. . . .

Around eight thirty Mr. Ball came to take me to
chapel. "How's our hero this morning?"

"Fine, sir. Did they find Mr. Woodrow?"

"They found him all right. He's just fine, son. I
reckon he'll be back at work tomorrow, and he'll
want to tell you the story himself. Too sore to go to
chapel?"

"No, sir. I might limp."

On the march to chapel, the air was fresh and cool
from the rain. The hill didn't look the same. A ray of
sunlight beamed down through a dark bank of
clouds.

"Boys, I'm here to tell you today, you can sink so

low in this life, so low. But you can't sink so low that the hand of Jesus can't reach down to lift you up. How can that be? Why, it's simple, friends. It's because your power to sin will never be as great as God's power to forgive. Your power to hate others will never be as great as His power to love you. Jesus is reaching his hand down to you today, friends. He wants to lift you up, and he wants you to accept his love. And when you do that, boys, your response to that gift of grace will be to want to lift up others and to love them as He loves you."

It was the Reverend Bacon, but no one was heckling. The news from the morning paper was buzzing around and had all the boys' attention. Every now and then, one of my table boys would look over and give me a smile or a thumbs-up. To me, the Reverend Bacon didn't look like a clown this morning.

As the service ended, I actually felt good in a way I hadn't felt since I was first sent up. But before we left the chapel, Mr. Ball got up to make an announcement. "Some of you boys may have heard about a newspaper article this morning. Mr. Palmer, whom you all know, and Mr. Silvy have been arrested for some very serious crimes. I just want to tell you boys that this trouble doesn't change your routine in any way. Extra staff has been called in to help ensure order, and order will be kept. This is a matter that does not concern you."

This is a matter that does not concern you? I thought. Evan was killed and Becka was kidnapped and Nose was getting sent off because of what Shorty Nub had been doing. How did that not concern me? As the others filed out, Mr. Ball kept me behind in the front pew. "Bowser, you sit here by me," he said.

I expected he wanted to give me a heartfelt thanks on behalf of the facility or something.

"Bowser, that was a fine thing you did, rescuing that girl."

"Thank you, sir."

"Sooner or later, some people from the sheriff's office or the Commonwealth's Attorney's office are going to want to talk with you. Are you ready for that?"

"I'll try to help in any way I can, Mr. Ball. There is one thing I'd like to ask, though."

"What is it, Bowser?"

"Sir, I can assure you that Nose had nothing to do with Evan's death. In fact, I think if you look into it, you'll find that the accident occurred because Shorty Nub left his post to commit these crimes. Nose getting blamed was part of the Nub's cover-up. I'd like to ask that Nose be sent back to Cottage B and that his transfer be dropped."

Mr. Ball was very businesslike. "I'm afraid we can't do that. The administration is in no mood to have troublemakers use this to stir up a lot of fuss."

I thought for a while before I got a glimmer of where this was going. "You don't want anybody asking about how Evan got killed."

"The important thing," he continued calmly, "is that we're going to get you out of here."

"What about Nose?" I asked.

"What about him?"

"You can't send him to Lorton now."

Mr. Ball was as relaxed as ever. "Nose's going to Lorton has nothing to do with the accident, or the events of yesterday, or you."

I was on my feet now.

"Sit down!" he ordered, but I ignored him.

"Nose was going to Lorton because the Nub wanted him to," I said. "It was all because the Nub wanted everybody to blame Nose so they wouldn't find out where the Nub was when Evan got killed."

Mr. Ball said, "Nose is being transferred to another more secure facility because the progress committee has seen a pattern of incorrigibility."

I just stood staring at him.

"Watch it, Bowser," he warned. "This can still get very hot for you."

"And how's that, Mr. Ball?" I asked.

"The progress committee could find that you've become incorrigible—"

"And send *me* to Lorton?" I asked.

"That's not all, Bowser. If the boys find out you

taped them to prove they were lying about the incident, it could get very bad for you in the cottage. Mr. Lindquist gave me that tape you made, and I listened to it. That's a dangerous thing, gathering evidence to use against people. You could get hurt badly. You should make extra sure in these troubled times that any piece of evidence you have comes to me before anyone else knows about it and that you do with it as I say. Do you understand?"

"No. I don't think I do. I don't understand why you won't stop Nose's transfer, and I don't understand why you're leaning all over me."

"Bowser, let Nose drop. He went at you twice. If I were you, I'd take care of myself and let Nose take care of himself."

"Is that what they taught you in church?" I asked. "'Thou shalt take care of yourself'? I may be nuts, and I may be an asshole, but I wouldn't let them take all the hope away from a good boy just for my own convenience. Nose won't break easily, and once he's broken, he won't be any use again."

"Well," he said, "you'd better watch your back until we can get you to that hospital."

"Wait a second!" I yelled. "Why the hell should I watch my back? I didn't rape any fourteen-year-olds!" I sat back down and tried to pull it all together. "Mr. Ball, listen to me for a minute. Nose and I worked in the school building, and I got to know him. He was never out to get me. In the shower, he fought me because he had to. When he hit me outside, it's because he wanted to stop me from messing myself up. I don't believe there's a mean bone in that boy's body."

"He attacked a staff member."

"I saw that and so did you. Shorty Nub provoked him. He kicked Nose full in the ass after Nose had already put his hands on his head."

I could tell that Mr. Ball was losing patience. "Bowser, I don't think you're getting my drift here. Let me make it simple for you. We can make things easy for you, or we can make things hard. If you give any evidence you have to me before anyone else is aware of it and do with it as I say, I can get you sent to that hospital for a while. When everything has blown over, I can see you get released from there. Hell, I'll even go a step farther. Once things have blown over, I can arrange to find that there was a misunderstanding about your boy Nose. I could bring him back here from Lorton and see that he serves an easy three months and is released.

"On the other hand, things could become very hard for you. For instance, I don't know what the boys here might do if they knew that one of them was taping the others, especially if they already knew that the informer was working with the police. I don't know what we could do to control them. We've never had such a dangerous situation before. It'd be even more dangerous if someone in the administration let the boys know that the informer had been making tapes for a while and had been cooperating with the administration on an ongoing basis.

"Another thing to keep in mind, Bowser, is that the folks who will be asking you questions will do their investigation and then move on. But I will remain here and hold influence over the progress committee. In other words, I'll continue to be able to make your life hell. We could decide that you really don't require treatment, and we could find it best for you to stay with us for quite a while, even until your eighteenth birthday, if you live that long.

"Then, of course, there is Nose. You were quite right in pointing out that our friends at Lorton could break him; after all, he has a bad temper. For that matter, as I mentioned, the progress committee could find that you, yourself, are incorrigible and arrange that you keep Nose company in Lorton.

"It's all very simple. You may turn any evidence you have over to me before you inform anyone else about it, and follow my instructions about whether or not to share that information and, if so, how. Things will then become very easy for you. If, however, you decide not to follow these instructions, things for you will become very difficult. It's up to you. Do you understand now?"

I finally realized how slow I was being on the uptake. For Mr. Ball, Nose was a side issue. His main object was to suppress evidence on Shorty Nub's crimes. I knew that waiting to think would show my hand, so I looked innocent and perplexed, but I answered right away. "Sir, I have no information beyond what the police would already have."

"That's fine, Bowser, as far as it goes, but how did you know where to find the girl?"

"I didn't. After I shot the hump, I waded way upstream to try to lose the dogs. I just happened on her there. She had gotten away somehow and saw me stealing Mr. Woodrow's boat."

"And how did Mr. Woodrow happen to be there?"

"It was a logical place to look for me, I guess, an abandoned shelter upstream of this place. Mr. Woodrow has lived around here all his life."

"And why, Bowser, did you steal Mr. Woodrow's boat only to bring it back here?"

"After the girl told me she'd been kidnapped, I figured I didn't need to run. If I rescued her and brought her back, I'd be a hero and you guys would forgive everything and cut my time." I paused hopefully. "That could still happen, Mr. Ball, couldn't it?"

"It could, Bowser, if you are really as smart as you pretend. One more thing, though. Did you pick up anything from that site? Anything at all?"

"No, sir," I said. "Why would I do that? I was just

trying to steal a boat. I didn't even know what was going on there until that girl flagged me."

Mr. Ball looked at me hard and doubtfully. "We must be getting back, Bowser."

We didn't say a word on the way back. Once I was in lockdown, I felt as though someone had hung me upside down in handcuffs and spun me. I was almost woozy and still ragged from shooting the hump. Before I could start spinning off into story time, though, I told myself that losing traction was not what this situation called for. Things were really happening to Nose, and he needed my help.

I closed my eyes, took a few deep breaths, and played back in my mind every single word that Mr. Ball had said to me. I worked it all over for meaning, and I asked myself, What does he want, and why does he want it?

By suppertime, I had come to a simple conclusion: Mr. Ball was a part of Shorty Nub's operation. He might not have wanted many questions asked about how Evan died just because of his responsibility as an administrator, but that wouldn't explain his interest in physical evidence from the site. What would he have known to be there that scared him so much? Maybe financial records. Then again, maybe other things. There were a film canister and photographs in Mr. Woodrow's live well.

It turned out to be a busy Sunday. Right after

supper Mr. Woodrow showed up, still with that same gentle smile. He sat down on the cot next to me and offered me a Pall Mall. Before even getting to Mr. Ball's game, I wanted to clear the air.

"Mr. Woodrow, I'm sorry as hell they took you away at gunpoint and I didn't do a damn thing to help."

Bowser dog, there ain't a thing you should've done different. If they'd've heard you climbing out the window, we likely both have been shotgunned. You did what I hoped you'd do. I just tried to steer them away from you so you could get that girl out of there and get to the sheriff.

I figured the reason they was so interested in my truck was they didn't want nobody to find it near their clubhouse. I reckoned they was going to drive it far away and maybe set it on fire with me dead in the cab, maybe even blame it on you. After I led them wrong for about ten miles, I pretended to be so scared that I forgot where it was. After a time, Shorty Nub got exasperated and just started telling me all the bad things they might do to me when we got back to camp.

When we got back to the scene of the crime, they hid their pickup truck off behind the broken-down cinder block shack. Silvy was holding the shotgun, and Shorty Nub pulled his cowboy Colt .45 revolver out from behind the seat and strapped on the holster. Then they looked everything over good and saw the girl was gone, somebody been up in the clubhouse through the window, and the crew they was supposed to meet had probably been there and gone. You must have taken off with the girl not long before.

They inspected the place pretty close, and found a 30-30 shell casing in the opening close to the bank. I was praying that if that shot had been for you, it missed you clean. Shorty Nub say to Silvy, "Take Woodrow yonder behind that woodshed and keep the shotgun on him. If the cops show up and you keep him quiet, they might go away. If they don't, we can use him as a hostage." The Nub went back to the truck for gasoline to start burning the clubhouse down.

I did my best shuffle over to the shed and eyed a long piece of two-by-four leaning up against it, and I started to work on Silvy right away. "Mr. Silvy," I say, "you been working with me for years. You know that I know how to have a good time as good as the next man. Seems to me, it'd be the best for the both of us if we was to work together. Look here. If them cops come up here and you take me for hostage, how do you reckon it's going to end? You know they going to shoot you or lock you up for good. Damn! Kidnapping, maybe murder, not to mention all the other bidness you all been up to (although that ain't none of my bidness)."

I say, "I jest come up here to look for Bowser dog, so I

192

could get some raise or a day off if I got him. Hell, I didn't have no way to know what y'all was up to. But now that I got the idea of it, I'll be honest with you, I wouldn't mind getting a little piece of that myself. Why, you could give me a little money from what you made and jest treat me like a guest of the house now and then for a drink of whiskey and a good time with the ladies. I'll be pleased to tell anybody we was all up here together to look for that boy that shot the hump." I could tell I had him when he smiled and shook his head at me.

"I bet you would like that, wouldn't you, Woodrow? Just what kind of money we talking about?"

"I don't reckon twenty grand would be out of bounds." When he started to laugh at what a stupid, greedy, horny, shiftless old nigger he's dealing with, he bowed his head and let the barrel of the shotgun drop. I didn't even bother to try to grab his gun. I just picked up that pine two-by-four and smacked him flat in the nose, like a baseball. When he was on his knees, I broke the board over his head. It was kind of like the Three Stooges, except with a lot more screaming and blood and bone showing. He wouldn't be standing up for a while, anyway. I grabbed that shotgun and stepped into the woods.

Shorty Nub done already set the clubhouse afire. He pulled out his Colt .45, and I hoped he was so stupid as to try to find me. Who wouldn't rather have a twelve-gauge than a pistol to shoot something moving in the woods? Besides, I seen the Nub showing off with that fancy shooting iron down in the field, and I'd be surprised if he could hit the ground if he was aiming at it.

I was half surprised he was smarter than that; but I didn't reckon he was much smarter. I reckoned he'd go to make some noise like he was going upstream until he was pretty sure I wasn't stalking him, and then he'd double back to get to his truck.

I just took my time and stepped along the bank and up to the other side of the truck. I sat leaning against the tire admiring the pretty Remington pump in my hand, checking how many shells was in it and what kind (there was four #00 buck). It seemed more like a bird gun than a deer gun to me, so it felt a little odd to have buck load in the chamber. But I had all the faith in the world that it'd work just fine on a deer within twenty yards. Or on a man, for that matter.

I settled down to relax quiet and waited to hear an asshole creep up through the brush. Sure enough, the Nub did make a terrible racket. When he was out in the open between the shack and the truck, I called to him, "Nub, you know I got a twelve-gauge shotgun and you got a pistol. How do you think you going to come out in a gunfight? Why don't you just lay that toy down and put your hands on your head, because if I see them anywhere else when I stand up from the bed of this here truck, I'm going to have to cut you down."

I lifted that barrel up behind the tailgate, and he was standing with his gun drawn like he was Billy the Negro Kid. He had not even brought that pistol to eye level, like this was a damn O.K. Corral shoot-out and he was going to shoot me from the hip. Plus, he really thought I was going to pop up from the bed. When he saw my muzzle, he shot fast three times but hit somewhere in Kentucky, I reckon. He was staring at the muzzle of the shotgun with that pistol smoking in his hand, and I think it come to him that I could cut him down no matter which way he tried to run.

"Throw down that pistol," I said. I was lying behind the rear wheel of the truck now, with the bead on him from under the bed.

He licked his lips and shot the other three bullets in the revolver but didn't hit any closer than the side panel of the truck bed. I stood up with the muzzle pointed right at his chest and walked up to six feet from him.

"Throw that pistol over here. Now throw me your truck keys."

He did, and he put his hands on his head without even being asked. He was licking his lips now and his green eyes was worried. I couldn't help but say to him, "Boss man, you dumber than you is mean."

When Deputy Sasser found us, Shorty Nub was kneeling in the dirt with his hands on his head, and I was sitting back in the truck listening to Al Green on the radio. The cab door was open so I could keep a bead on the

Nub. The deputy stepped out of his car with his police shotgun and walked over to the truck.

"Would you mind turning down that radio? Are you Ernest Woodrow?"

"Yes, sir."

"Lay your firearm on the ground, please, and step over to my car."

"I'll put down the shotgun, but you keep a bead on this man. He's a kidnapper and worse. He'd kill both of us if he could."

I should have reckoned he'd heard some of the story from you and the girl. He put the Nub in handcuffs, walked him to the car, and locked him into the back seat with the cage in front of him. The Nub kept his mouth shut but was looking mean again. I told the deputy where Silvy was lying with a headache and a broken nose. By that time another deputy got there. I sat with Sasser in the front seat back to his station. After they locked the Nub up, the deputy come back to the office and asked me questions. I told him everything just as it happened. Almost.

· 13 ·

CORPUS DELICTI

MR. WOODROW GOT SERIOUS and looked straight at me with eyes the color gold in a cat's-eye stone. He bobbed his thumb toward the door. "Bowser, I wanted to tell you, after all that excitement yesterday, I went to fishing and then watched a movie after supper." He raised his eyebrows until I figured out that he was talking about the film canister I put in his bait well. I nodded my head to show I understood. "Yeah, a kung fu movie about a guy named Master Ball." I figured he meant that Mr. Ball was in that film. "Have you seen that movie yet? No, of course you ain't. You ain't going to take no one to the movies until you and Nose both get *off this Hill*, are you?"

Then he stopped still and looked in my eyes. I had never seen him before without a smile on his lips, but he was no longer able to erase the smile creases around his eyes. "Well, Bowser dog, I reckon I better get on up home now and take a nap. I'm too damned old for all this monkey bidness."

Next morning after breakfast Mr. Ball came to get me to talk with a detective from the sheriff's office. On the way Mr. Ball said, "Don't forget what we talked about yesterday."

Even with this threat looming, the worst part was just captivity. The rainstorm had entirely passed. It was a bit of relief getting out of lockdown, seeing the trees in the distance, junglelike from the heat and rain, and feeling the sun and the breeze. I hated lock-down more than ever since I shot the hump. I was sick of being in a cage. I could feel confinement in my chest like a hand that could squeeze my heart until it burst. I didn't know how Nose could stand it so long without beating himself to death against a wall. I wanted to get back to the cottage, but it wasn't some-thing I hoped for. I couldn't wish for a bigger cage, especially with Nose still locked down. I didn't know how I could stand not being free another day, and I knew things were likely to get worse before they got better. I needed to focus, and I tried to focus on saving Nose.

We went to that same room where I'd sat with Dr. Garcia. A young man with a strong jaw and brown eyes greeted me with a dimpled smile that even put me at ease. He was lean and muscular but dressed funny. He had on a short-sleeved shirt that seemed too short for his long upper arms and a goofy tie with a picture of a fish on it. He was not at all my idea of a detective, more like a hockey coach.

"Hey, Richard. I'm Deputy Sasser, but you can call me Cal if you like."

"Cal Sasser! Deputy Sasser, you're Miss Lovitt's boyfriend!"

His dimples got even deeper. "Yeah, she told me a good bit about you. You like some of my favorite books," he said.

"Man, you are lucky! She is a fine woman. I hope she's not pissed at me shooting the hump in her car."

"Nah." He waved in the air in a gesture that was almost athletic. "Daffy has insurance. She was just glad you saved that girl and that you're safe. She got her wallet back."

"Daffy?"

"Her real name is Daphne. Well," he said, and pulled out a steno pad, "we'd better get on with the show." I got the impression that he wouldn't have minded just chatting about Miss Lovitt if he didn't have work to do.

He didn't sit behind the desk. We sat facing each other in cheap easy chairs.

"Deputy Sasser, I don't mean to be rude, but I can't tell you anything." He looked both annoyed and curious, waiting for me to explain. "I can't talk now, or here, or to you."

"Well then. When, and where, and to whom?" he asked.

"Off the Hill, to the DA."

"Richard, we don't have a DA in Virginia. We call him the Commonwealth's Attorney."

"Okay then. The Commonwealth's Attorney. But off the Hill."

He remained calm. "In circumstances like this, that may not be unreasonable. The problem is that you've already escaped once—and stolen a car to do it. The Commonwealth's Attorney's going to think you might try again." We were both quiet for a minute. "Richard, did you see any evidence that could be used against these people?"

"Yes."

"Will you be willing to testify against them?"

"Yes."

"Do you know the whereabouts of any physical evidence that can be used against these people?"

"Yes. One other thing: Don't let Mr. Ball take me off the Hill. Send an escort from the state to get me."

I looked at that oil painting above the desk while I waited for him to respond: a white dog in mid motion, running through hills of green and brown.

"Do you like the painting?" Deputy Sasser asked.

"I like the way the white dog draws the hills to a point."

"That's Daffy's."

"You mean she painted it?"

"Yeah," he said proudly. "It's on loan to the school."

When Mr. Ball came to get me, he made small talk with Sasser for a minute, doing his hail-fellow-well-met routine that he does so well, ending with a friendly hand on my shoulder.

"Now that Richard is rested and well fed, we'll take him back to his cottage." I was happy to hear it at first, but as we walked up the hill, I started to have my doubts.

Before we reached Cottage B, I said, "I didn't tell him anything, Mr. Ball, but Deputy Sasser told me that the Commonwealth's Attorney would want to talk to me." Mr. Ball just glared at me.

I got a hero's welcome at the cottage. I had shot the hump and come back. Everyone was asking me questions.

Before we lined up for supper, Mr. Lindquist called Babybird out. He was gone about a half hour, but got back in time for chow. I was going to tell the long story that night at the dinner table, but by that time no one would talk to me.

Finally I asked, "What the hell is wrong with you guys?"

Snicklesnort said, "Nothing. We just don't want our conversation taped."

I asked, "What are you talking about?"

Babybird answered, "We're talking about Mr. Ball playing a tape of me talking with you."

Snicklesnort said, "Did you ever hear what we do around here to informers? This one boy, they gagged him with a pillowcase and held him down with his legs spread. Then they shafted him with a broom stick until he was bleeding, then they kicked a football into his balls until blood was coming out of his mouth. We're going to think of something even better for you."

Fear began to pass over me, but I refused it. I cast it from me like a demon, and I remembered Nose. "I didn't tape that to get anybody in trouble other than Shorty Nub," I said. "You guys didn't do anything wrong, and neither did Nose. I just want to keep him from going to Lorton."

"So you're taping Babybird and showing us up as liars to stand up for that flat-nosed black bastard?"

"That's right. So what are you going to do about it?" I said.

Snickle was seething. "You're going to see what we'll do."

Babybird and Ben Susan were staring on me with unbelieving hatred.

After supper, I took a book and sat on a chair

under the stairs. Every time a white boy got near me, he'd try to kick me or punch me. The black boys stared at me with contempt. Apparently the story had gotten all around. I knew I was in danger, but I felt confident and almost calm. I felt like a showdown was coming that would somehow bring everything to a head, like a thunderstorm, and wash all Hill time and story time away. I wanted to take them all on.

I decided to start it in the dorm, before they could come up with a plan or come by weapons. The garrote was still hidden under the stoop at the library, but that couldn't be used against more than one person taken by surprise. I wouldn't have wanted to use it on anyone but the Nub anyway.

After Mr. Lindquist had marched us to our bunks and locked us in, I got down off my bunk and walked to the end of the dorm where no one would be able to get behind me. They always kept it pretty bright in there so the night men could see that we were all in our bunks. I stood there between the bunks and called out, "Snicklesnort, you guys are all a bunch of pussies."

Everyone was excited. Not only was I taking on the whole cottage, but it was only a matter of minutes before the night men would look in, and it was sure to get brutal.

Snickle said, "Ben Susan, Babybird, let's take him down."

All three of them came down the aisle. Snick-lesnort had his hands out, not fisted, but like a wrestler, the way he always fought. I was motioning him to come on while I was talking. "That's right; I taped Babybird telling about Evan. I taped it to keep Nose from going to Lorton." I was saying this mostly to Gray, who was watching all this from the top bunk next to me.

Snickle said, "We got to put this Mad Dog down." He came in to try to grab my shirt. Ben Susan and Babybird were behind him, waiting to jump on after Snickle pulled me down. I blocked his hand and punched him in the throat with my left hand. He fell back, and Ben Susan tackled me by the leg. I fell on top of Ben Susan and got him in a headlock, but that took both hands, and Babybird kicked my ribs. Snicklesnort was coming back to hold me down when suddenly Gray was off his bunk and on the ground. You could tell he had been waiting for this moment. Maybe he had dreamed of something like this every time he worked out.

He was smiling, standing above me with his big shoulders squared, and he said, "If you don't keep your hands off that boy, I'm going to tear you apart."

Ben Susan and Babybird hung back, but Snickle came on like he was going to kick me where I was kneeling. Gray stepped into him and caught him upside the head with a wide, hard right. You could hear Snickle's jaw crack, and then the night men were yelling in the window.

"Stop it now! Everyone's hands on their heads!" Two rednecks with baseball caps—one fat with a beard and one skinny and clean-shaven—unlocked the door and strode in with big flashlights like truncheons in their hands.

The older, skinny one walked up to Snickle and said, "Who did this to you?" Snickle's face was a mess. I don't think he could have talked if he wanted to, but he didn't want to. The skinny redneck took a close look at Snickle's cheek and said to the other, "We're going to have to get this one to the hospital."

Then the younger, fat man grabbed Babybird by the arm and shook him. "Who started this?" Babybird's eyes were desperate, shifting from Snickle to Gray. The fat man took his flashlight and whacked Babybird right in the belly and Babybird fell to his knees. They stood over him like they were waiting to hit him again.

As soon as he got his breath back, Babybird said, "It was Bowser"—nodding his head toward me— "He's been going down for the black boys, and we couldn't stand it. Snickle pulled Bowser out of a colored boy's bunk and Bowser slugged him."

Both of the rednecks walked over and stood one on either side of me. "OOOH! You a pretty boy, ain't you?" said the fat one.

"You like that dark meat, don't you, faggot?" the skinny man taunted.

"Answer the man, sissy!" said the fat man, sticking his big bearded face right into mine and shoving his flashlight between my legs. For the first time I spoke the psalm aloud.

> O Lord my God, in thee do I take refuge;
> save me from all my pursuers, and deliver me,
> lest like a lion they rend me, dragging me away,
> with none to rescue.

The two night men stood quiet for a moment, until the fat one said, "You queer and crazy ain't you?"

Just then Mr. Lindquist came into the room barefoot, with no shirt. He walked up to the two night men with his back ramrod straight and said, "I'll take it from here, men. Go back on your patrol."

The fat man started to protest. "They was starting a riot in here."

"I SAID, RESUME YOUR PATROL, GENTLEMEN!"

It looked like they wanted to defy him, but they backed down. "Well," said the fat man, "you can have them."

Mr. Lindquist called Mr. Franklin in to take a look at Snickle. I heard later that an ambulance came and took him to the hospital. Snickle never told who hit him or even that he'd been hit. He kept saying he fell out of bed.

Mr. Lindquist didn't try to get the story out of anybody in the dorm, but he decided right off that I needed to get locked down. On the way over to lockdown he asked, "What was that about?"

"Like you don't know," I said. "I can't believe you would do this. I gave you that tape in confidence."

"What are you talking about?" he asked.

"I'm talking about Mr. Ball playing that tape for Babybird."

Mr. Lindquist looked more pissed off than I'd ever seen him, but he didn't say anything.

They put me in the lockdown room down the hall from Nose. When Mr. Lindquist was gone, I kicked my door and shouted, "Nose, homeboy! Steady man."

Next morning after a half-portion breakfast I heard the keys in the door and it was Mr. Woodrow. "Well, Bowser dog, you do know how to get into things, don't you?"

"I reckon I do," I said.

"This here is something from Miss Lovitt." He handed me a Bible. "She wrote a note for you inside the front cover," he said.

We smoked a fog together, and he said, "Hang in there now." Then he went down the hall to visit a little with Nose. I found the note on a small sheet of paper inside the front cover of the Bible.

> *I am contacting Evan's mother to get her to push for an inquiry. If anyone asks you any questions, let on that you have extensive information about Evan's death as well as Palmer's sex ring, but REFUSE TO TELL ANYONE ANYTHING UNTIL THEY GET YOU AND NOSE OFF THE HILL FOR PROTECTION.*
>
>

God bless you,
Daffy Lovitt

>
> *Flush this note.*

I flushed it.

The very next morning I heard a key in the door. A man in shirt and tie came in and sat on the bunk next to me. "My name is Mr. Frybourne. I am an assistant to the Commonwealth's Attorney, Mr. Wineberg. A driver from Juvenile Justice is going to take you over to the county courthouse, where we are going to meet with Mr. Wineberg. Deputy Sheriff Sasser and Mr. Ball, the Belmont residency director, will also be in the meeting. We'll be asking you some questions. Your cooperation is very important to us. If you cooperate, it will be noted in your file and may influence the progress committee positively in determining your dispensation. On the other hand, if you do not cooperate, that may have a negative impact. Do you understand?"

"Yeah, I understand. Now you listen. I am going with you to this meeting, and I would love to tell you everything I know about Evan's death and about Palmer's crimes—and it is a very good story. However, unless you get me the hell off this hill and get James Braxton off, too, I ain't telling squat. I don't even remember how to speak English. I would prefer to keep my juvenile ass intact and to continue to breathe, regardless of the progress committee's determination regarding my dispensation. Do you understand?"

Mr. Frybourne looked at me as though he would like to squash me. "Well, Richard, I can't promise you that we will be able to move you, but that's something we can discuss with Mr. Ball."

"It's Mr. Ball who doesn't want me telling my story," I said. "I wouldn't expect him to protect me."

Mr. Frybourne looked mildly interested. "We'll discuss this with Mr. Wineberg at any rate."

Mr. Wineberg, Mr. Frybourne, Deputy Sasser, and Mr. Ball were already seated and chatting when I was led into the room. Mr. Wineberg studied me closely and asked me to take a seat. He had a thick head of gray hair and was pretty fat, but sitting back in his suspenders with no jacket, he looked like he would be at home anywhere. Once we were seated, he said, "We would like to ask you some questions about events that happened on the day you escaped. Is that all right with you?"

"You can ask me any questions you want, but I'm not saying a word unless you get me and James Braxton off the Hill."

Mr. Wineberg leaned over the table at me, and all the folksy manner was gone. His face and voice were hard. "Boy, I don't think you grasp the seriousness of this situation."

"Sir, I don't mean any disrespect, but I don't think you grasp the seriousness of my situation. I believe I would be in danger if I were to stay at Belmont after talking with you."

Mr. Ball rolled his eyes. "Ben," he said to Mr. Wineberg, "don't let this boy jerk you around. As you know, these boys can be very good at manipulation, and this boy here is probably as good as they get."

Deputy Sasser jumped in. "Mr. Wineberg, I believe that the boy could have a legitimate concern about his safety. I think you should hear him out."

Mr. Ball looked at Deputy Sasser like he was nuts, then shook his head with his hands over his eyes, theatrical.

Mr. Wineberg looked down at his notes. "You recently ran from Belmont and stole a car from a staff person?"

"Yes, sir."

"And according to your file you have been diagnosed with emotional disturbance so severe that you need hospitalization. It looks to me like you're a pretty high-risk juvenile. I'm not even sure how much value your testimony would have as a witness. I can't help but wonder if this information you say you have isn't just a bluff to get you out of Belmont." Then he paused for a long time, looking at his notes again. Finally he said, "Richard, help me out here. Unless you can give me some reason to believe you really know something, I'm inclined to send you back under Mr. Ball's care."

Mr. Ball burst in here, exasperated. "Ben, let me take him back to the Hill. I'll be able to get the whole story out of him without having to waste your time."

Deputy Sasser said to Mr. Wineberg, "I think you should hear the boy out."

It didn't look to me like this was going well, but I thought of something. "Mr. Wineberg, I can't tell you what I know, but I can tell you some questions that I can help you answer."

"Ben, don't let him pull this on you," said Mr. Ball.

Mr. Wineberg paused for a moment, then turned to me. "Okay, tell me the questions."

"One," I said, "what were those men doing in the deer camp? I can show you exactly, with physical evidence. Two, what part did Mr. Ball have in it? Three, where was Mr. Palmer at the time of the accident that killed Evan? Four, is James Braxton being sent to Lorton because he knows more about the accident than some people want him to tell?"

"What part Mr. Ball had in what? I'm not aware of him being implicated in anything."

Mr. Ball leaped up from the table. "This is absurd. This boy needs help."

Mr. Wineberg thought for a moment, trying to figure out what I might be talking about. "Evan Holister? I don't see the connection." Then: "Richard, you weren't even there when Evan Holister died. Who is James Braxton? You're not making a lot of sense."

My veins felt like they would burst, and I began to fear that maybe the truth was too hot for even Mr. Wineberg to touch. I drew what I thought might be my last card. "Have you heard the tape that Mr. Ball holds on which a boy recounts what really happened on the day Evan was killed? If not, why hasn't Mr. Ball played it for you?"

Mr. Ball broke in. "You little punk."

Mr. Wineberg raised his voice. "Bob, do you have a tape like that?"

Mr. Ball was blubbering. "Of course not."

I prayed silently my prayer for deliverance.

O Lord my God, in thee do I take refuge;
save me from all my pursuers, and deliver me,
lest like a lion they rend me, dragging me away,
with none to rescue.

The next play occurred to me like an answer to that prayer. I had no other card to draw, but I could bluff. I didn't know anything about how Mr. Lindquist had handed over the tape to Mr. Ball. I didn't even know if Mr. Lindquist had listened to it. But if I could make Mr. Ball think that Mr. Lindquist still held a copy, if I could get him to wonder or doubt even for a minute, I might be able to flush him out.

"Mr. Wineberg, if you talk to Mr. Lindquist, the B cottage housefather, I think he can provide a copy of that tape, and he can confirm that he gave the tape to Mr. Ball."

Mr. Wineberg looked at Mr. Ball like he would stare him down if he felt like it, and it wouldn't be a bit of effort. He said, "Bob?"

"Well, yes, Ben, yes. Mr. Lindquist gave me a tape, but I forgot all about it. I don't think it is of any consequence."

Mr. Wineberg looked deadly. "Don't you think you should let me be the judge of that?"

Mr. Ball drew himself up in scorn. "Ben, this boy is trying to whip you around. All he wants to do is

213

get off the Hill, and he's playing us against each other. Like you said, the boy's already tried to run and stolen a car. Not only that, but he's got serious mental problems. Why, he wasn't even there when that accident occurred. Leave him to me; I'll get out of him whatever he has to tell."

Mr. Wineberg was wiping off his bifocals. "Ball, you just had a death at your facility that occurred on the watch of one of your direct reports who has been arrested for kidnap, rape, and child abuse. Now you think I'm going to just hand this problem over to you to handle as you see fit? I'll be frank with you. I think we have already given you too much to handle as you see fit, and children may have suffered or died for it. This boy may have risked his life to save that girl, and I think we can give him a chance to tell us what he knows.

"Frybourne," Mr. Wineberg continued, "I want you to make a phone call to arrange an immediate transfer of Richard to the Juvenile Diagnostic Center."

"What about James Braxton?" I asked. "Sir, I can't talk with him still on the Hill. It might put him in danger."

Wineberg said to Mr. Frybourne, "Call to arrange transportation to the Diagnostic Center for Mr. Braxton within the hour."

"What if the Diagnostic Center isn't ready to accept them?" Frybourne asked.

"Then find somewhere else to put them. However you do it, make sure that Braxton is out of that facility within an hour and that Richard here does not go back to that facility."

Cal Sasser looked steadily at Mr. Ball and said, "Why don't you come down to the Sheriff's office with me? I'd like to ask you some questions."

"Ben!" Mr. Ball protested.

But Mr. Wineberg didn't have to think even a minute. He didn't even look at Mr. Ball. He said, "Thank you, Deputy Sasser," and began to collect his papers.

· 14 ·

A BIRD IN THE BUSH

IT'S ALWAYS A CLEAN white car. It's always a young man who drives it, a student of social work or corrections. We get to the river and cross it. Then cornfields and pastures roll on the opposite side of the glass like a movie. There never has been a Hill time; there will never be Hill time, no progress. Somehow, real people have crept into story time.

Characters I will never see again live in my story time, people like Shorty Nub and Mr. Greenjeans whose shadows will remain with me like masks of the devil, constant reminders of the presence and purity of evil; people like Snicklesnort and Ben Susan, Babybird, Gray, Mr. Lindquist, each with an endless number of possible ends, none of them blocked by events outside the story's loop of time. Mr. Woodrow and Miss Lovitt live there, too, who saved me by teaching me to want to save somebody else; and Evan, frozen innocent by death. Nose I will see again, and his future in story time is certain to me, to be the store man who will give food to the poor and write it in a big book with a sharp pencil.

At the Diagnostic Center, they put Nose and me in different cottages at first, so they could take depositions from us separately without our being able to compare notes. They made Nose into a student counselor, and he helped the housefathers supervise the kids. We'd give each other skin when we passed in the dining hall, and one of us would whoop, "What you doing, man?"

And the other, "Nothing but time, man, nothing but time."

The rec room of my cottage in the Diagnostic Center had a high ceiling and cinder block walls painted orange and plenty of light. I staked out the piano bench to sit back on and read. The piano blocked me off from the common area and made a little nest. But I hung out a lot, too. I'd come out and sit at different tables and play hearts or tell stories.

Story time: harms and the child, crime and punishment, great escapes. We told stories to each other, and where we ran out of the truth we stretched it, and when we couldn't stretch the truth any more, we did without.

Mr. Frybourne came almost every day to listen to me tell a story. In it things were either true or not true: a thing either happened or didn't happen; a person did something or didn't. Each detail had a particular use, like a material for building a house. What he was building was a case, and I handed him the building blocks with precision, exactly as I had witnessed them. Not all of them though. Somewhere in the process it occurred to me that I should hold a few key details to myself, in case I needed them later on.

Frybourne usually came to the cottage to get me at about ten in the morning. He walked me over to the admin building, and we sat in orange plastic chairs at a table. It was September now, and the fields out the mesh window were ripening to a sweet gold.

By the middle of October, Frederick Palmer, Roy Silvy, Beverly Silvy, and Robert Ball had all been called before a grand jury.

As soon as the depositions were over, I asked to be moved to Nose's cottage, and they moved me. We were glad to see each other, and that first evening I asked him what I'd been wondering about for months.

"Nose," I asked, "you never got around to telling me what you did to get sent up. How about finishing your story?" Nose looked thoughtful.

"Did I tell you about the ducks?"

"Yes, Nose, you did."

The other kids at the table were dying to know

what he was talking about, but nobody dared inter-
rupt us.

"How about getting run over by the train?"

Some kid started to chuckle, until he saw that we
were still serious.

"Yeah, homeboy, you told me about getting run
over by the train."

Nose ruminated.

━━━━━━

Well, I come to on the tracks when I heard Officer
Remy say, "Great God almighty," and opened my eyes to
look straight into his eyes. Just then I felt like I been sent
back to do something in this world. The officer say,
"Hold still, boy, until we can get the EMTs up here," and
I just lay back looking at the full moon and feeling myself
alive.

The EMTs was hot to do something about my nose, so
I finally had to tell them a couple times, "It's been like
that for more than a year," and explain that I got my nose
broke in a fight and it just healed that way. At the hospital, they couldn't even find a bruise on me. Officer Remy
come around and asked, "James, do you remember what
happened before you passed out?" He had to repeat it,
loud. I could still hardly hear for the blowing up in my
ears.

"It felt like I died," I said.

"Do you remember your friend falling on the tracks?"

I closed my eyes and I could see the moonlight and I could hear Smiley scream. When I watched it all like a movie, I knew for the first time, I saved somebody's life.

Officer Remy bowed his head a little and said clear and solemn, "Ain't no greater love than for a man to give his life for a friend."

———

When Nose stopped, all of us at the table sat quiet and astonished, including me.

Finally I thought to say, "I still don't get it, Nose. Why'd they send you up?"

"I guess I could ask the same question of you, couldn't I?" he said.

"Go on and finish the story."

"I done told enough. You ain't told me nor no one else what you got sent up for, and I ain't telling you nothing else until you tell."

All the boys moaned with disappointment, but we got called to showers before they could plead with him.

Next day, everyone was on my back until I knew I'd never hear the end of it if I didn't tell my story. I went over it carefully in my head, and I kept putting everyone off until after dinner. When we were all around a big table, I still kept saying I was a victim of circumstance and strung them along as far as I could.

But I finally said, "I tell you what, Nose, you finish your story first, then I promise I'll tell mine."

Nose looked at me sideways and asked, "Swear?"

"Swear," I said.

———

When they let me go home from the hospital, Mumma come to get me. "James, I didn't raise you to run with a gang, drinking wine and stealing ducks. Plus, how did I raise a boy so dim-witted he get run over by a damn train?" She acted like she'd have dragged me out by my ear if I was little. But I could see she was proud. If she'd have let loose, she wasn't going to do nothing but cry like a baby and hug and kiss me to death.

Officer Remy told Mumma he had to give me a summons to go to court, but he told me and Mumma that he'd do what he could to get me off, seeing as how I saved a boy's life. Everybody treated me nice for the two weeks before trial. Smiley was always following me around and kept telling everybody, even strangers, about how I saved his life. A reporter for the *Petersburg Pilot* even came to ask me questions and wrote a article about the whole thing.

When we went to court, the Commonwealth's Attorney read off the charges: theft, vandalism, drinking under age. After about a hour, they done called up the Indian guy from the Scotty Mart and all the cops that had gone to check out the burglar call, and put together everything to make the case and put me away.

Then the lawyer they gave me took over. He called Officer Remy to the stand and started to put the story together by askin' him questions. The lawyer started out, "On the night of August 4, 1967—tell the court how you came to find the defendant on the railroad tracks near the Scotty Mart." And Remy told the whole story from what he saw.

"Officer," my lawyer asked him, "what do you believe would've become of this young boy (pointing to Smiley), if James Braxton had not pulled him from them tracks?"

Remy frowned. "He'd surely have been made into hamburger meat."

"And when James Braxton put hisself in front of that train, what would you say was his chances to survive?"

"One in a million, I'd say."

"So officer, are you saying that James Braxton tried to *lay down his life* to save his friend?"

Remy was so choked up, he couldn't answer. He pulled out a hanky and finally was able to say, "No greater love hath any man than to give his life for his friend."

I tell you there wasn't a dry eye in the court. I was even ready to bawl. The judge dropped the charges and asked me to go up to shake his hand and wished me good luck.

Mumma had to go back to work, so she give me five

dollars and told me to grab a bite to eat and take a bus home. After she took off, I catched up with Roberto and Simple on the courthouse steps.

Roberto say, "Okay, hero, let's go celebrate."

And Simple say, "Yeah, I'll buy you a bottle of wine, even if you did save my knucklehead little brother."

It was breezy and clear and blue and not so hot as it been. We got somebody to buy us a gallon of Mother Vineyard Scuppernong. Then we found us a fallen tree to sit on in a vacant lot behind the courthouse, and we just sat there looking at the courthouse through the trees, chugging wine and telling little bits of the story of the duck hunt, and the wine raid, and the train wreck, and the courtroom drama. Before long we was falling off that log, laughing.

Cutting up there, with breezes blowing through the poplars and me a hero and everything going to my head, was sure enough heaven and a bottle of wine. It was late afternoon when we pulled ourselves together to head back home. We started to kind of swaying along that street to the bus stop, and I felt like a angel.

We passed by a brick building full of lawyers' offices, and in the parking lot we spotted a bright red Cadillac convertible with cream vinyl seats. All three of us was admiring it when Roberto say, "Damn, the keys is in it!"

Simple looked around and opened the driver's seat door for me and say, "Your chariot done swung down."

And it seemed right. I felt like I was a angel from

heaven that nobody would mind me driving their Cadillac, even though I ain't drove but once before in my life.

I was doing okay until a patrol car pulled out right in front of the courthouse. I got scared and tried to put on the brakes but missed and hit the gas pedal. I'd say we got up to fifty miles a hour before we whacked into the back of that cop car. We knocked that vehicle right up off the curb and into a fire hydrant.

Nobody got hurt, but Officer Remy jumped out with his gun in both hands and creeped through the hydrant spray like a sailor trying to make it across the deck of a ship in a storm, right up to my window. I smiled at him, but he didn't smile back. He looked pale, then like he was going to get sick. They threw me right into the county jail, and when I sobered up, I was more embarrassed than anybody.

This time when I went to court, the very next day after they let me go for stealing wine, nobody seemed to remember me pulling Smiley from in front of that train. My lawyer didn't even look at me. When he called Officer Remy to the stand, Remy didn't look at nobody; he was ashamed. The judge said, "Belmont," and even my mumma sat satisfied with her arms crossed.

———

Everyone around the table was quiet for a while after that. We didn't know whether we should be laughing, and Nose didn't help us figure it out. He was looking at his hands.

Finally he raised his head. That crooked smile had come back.

———

But before they carried me up here, Mumma did come to see me.

"Son," she say, "even a pea-brain like you can see that God didn't save you just to steal a Cadillac. I believe he still has a plan for you, and I'll be waiting right here to see you come back and carry it out. Here, take this, to remember who you is."

———

"And she handed me this paper here." Nose pulled out a worn piece of composition paper from his pocket, unfolded it, and read:

Romans 8:18
For I reckon that the sufferings of this present time are not worthy to be compared with the glory which shall be revealed in us.

Nose looked around at all of us then, as though he'd told a joke and he wanted to see if we got it. Everybody was asking him questions and talking about Nose's story until it was just about time for showers, but Nose made me swear again, in front of everyone, that I would tell my story the next night after supper.

When the time came, I let myself drift back and told the whole story as if I were watching it happen.

―――――

Bradley Davis was the best storyteller in town. Every Sunday evening, he'd gather a whole crowd around him at a street corner for stories about the weekend. He always acted them out, with voices and sound effects, and he had hook lines in them like, "Cop comes around the corner. . . ." He was one of those kids with smarts he didn't show to adults. He was a greaser in his own movie who started fights too easily and got beaten too often. Still, you could usually see where he was headed and count on him to keep going that way.

I didn't think Bradley Davis was going to rob the store even though I saw him getting ready to do it. If I had thought it was real, I could have stopped him, but it was like being in a dream at the time. I wish I could roll the film back and do it over again.

I was holding some windowpane acid, hanging out at the Paragon Pharmacy. It was a mild spring Friday night, and nobody was around until Bradley Davis finally drove up. I told him I had some acid, and he said he'd take one hit if I took one with him. We each swallowed one and decided to go see an old detective movie, *The Big Sleep*. As I was getting off during the movie, I was thinking about how everything happened as reactions between poles: plus and minus, strong and weak, light and dark.

When we got out of the movie I tried to describe this to Bradley Davis, but he was on a whole different trip. He was playing a gangster and seemed to think he'd found his true identity. Then he pulled the car over and went around to the trunk. When he got back in the car, he had a .38 revolver in his pants under his denim jacket. I cracked up because he seemed to think he looked like Philip Marlowe when he really looked like a sixteen-year-old suburban kid with acne. The whole thing was hilarious to me, and he looked so silly I couldn't believe he could do anything.

He said, "Let's knock off the Paragon."

I answered in a dime-store gangster voice. "Right, Lefty. Let's shake him down for the loot then get the low-down on the dame so if we go over, the case won't stick with the DA and we can take it on the lam." Then I cracked up laughing.

You couldn't sway Bradley Davis by laughing at him. He handed the pistol to me to look at, and that was the first time I'd ever touched one. The crosscut of the matte on the handle fit into my hand like a girl's breast, and the nerves in my back tingled at the blue-steel cylinder clicking out and to. The trigger was a fulcrum between poles: soft and loud, life and death, good and evil. But it was only a toy to me. I handed it back to Bradley, and we took off down Franklin Street.

The Paragon Pharmacy had booths and a lunch counter, and behind the counter stood a cutout of a waitress in a frilly hat and checked apron with words coming out of her mouth: "It's fun to eat out." I went over to the magazine counter and was amusing myself with a *True Detective* magazine in a yellow flood from the fluorescent lights that I could feel all around me and right into my belly.

When I heard the two shots, the light started to flood red, and I ran toward the bangs not knowing why except to save Bradley Davis. I came around the corner, and Mr. Rupe stood holding his .38 in both hands; Bradley Davis lay on the floor. Red pooled on his chest and a froth of blood from the lung bubbled over his lip.

Mr. Rupe said to him, "Move and you're a dead man."

Bradley Davis managed to whisper, "I am a dead man."

Mr. Rupe looked proud when he turned to me and made me lie facedown with my hands above my head, right there next to Bradley Davis on the floor in his blood.

I was still tripping when they took me to jail. I shook all over as they strip-searched me, and the wardens started making cracks about me being queer. In the cell at first I thought I could channel the mass of my body through the bars into my hand and get out, but I didn't try.

Near dawn I started coming down. I could still see Bradley Davis on the floor, and hear him whisper, "I am a dead man." Then I thought about my parents. I didn't know what they would do—kill themselves, maybe. Or maybe my mom would have an attack of nerves, or my dad would have to go out of town on business.

When my dad showed up the next day he said, "You've really gotten yourself into it this time, haven't you?" I looked at the floor of the cell with nothing to say. "All we can do is figure out how to get you out of it."

Dad did his best for me, too. He hired the only lawyer he knew, who turned out to be a real estate attorney. I was lucky they didn't declare me an adult. Although, after I learned that Bradley Davis was really dead, I didn't care what they did to me.

Some of the boys liked any story with a robbery and a killing in it. One of them said, "You should've had a gun. Then you could have shot the store guy." Nose's eyes threatened the boy, and he shut up.

Everyone got quiet after that, and Nose said to me, "Bowser, I know you didn't mean for that boy to die."

I said, "I don't know how much what I meant matters. I gave him the acid, and I didn't even try to stop him from robbing the drugstore."

After that, whole crowds would gather around

when the two of us started telling stories about Belmont. I must admit we remembered new details all the time, and some of them we didn't even notice while they were happening.

So Nose and I are the VIPs of the place. We've been up the Hill and have returned to tell about it. It's almost like we died and came back to life. Plus, the other kids see how tight we are, like brothers, and it carries a lot of power.

Becka is here at the Diagnostic Center now. Of course, the girls and boys live in separate cottages and hardly ever get to talk. Becka and I have been looking at each other and smiling in the dining hall, which, of course, has led to a lot of razzing and crude humor from the other boys.

Yesterday was a mild, sunny October day, and they took us out on the field to play baseball. The girls and boys were on separate diamonds, but we were waiting for our turn at bat along the same foul line. I asked the cottage father if I could talk with Becka and he said yes, but no touching and keep the conversation appropriate.

Autumn folded Becka in, her hair blending with the color of the leaves. I was proud I'd saved her, and she wasn't at all ungrateful. She knew a lot of Dylan by heart. She recited a good bit of "Subterranean Homesick Blues," and I didn't know anyone could make it sound so sweet. She said she liked Rod McKuen, for which I was sorry, but when I listened to her voice, I thought I could even forgive her for that. She had some drawings with her, all freestyle and all of horses.

I caught a hoppergrass while we were talking and made a paper container to hold him in. She drew a picture of the hoppergrass as we talked. Then neither of us could think of anything to say until I finally asked, "Becka, what are you thinking about?"

Becka said, "You." Her voice was like the wrapping on a package that contained some precious gift. Before we got called to line up, she told me she had gotten a release date, and they were sending her back to live with her mom in Ashland, not too far from Richmond.

They always say that if you meet a girl in the joint, you'll never see her again on the street, but I've been thinking about Becka all day. Maybe this is different. I brought that hoppergrass in, and they let Nose keep him in a jar. I gave him Becka's hoppergrass drawing, too. Then, today, Nose got his release date.

It's been nearly eight months now since I first got sent up. I haven't seen or read the news much, but in the Diagnostic Center they let us stay up in the dorm one night to watch Neil Armstrong on TV, stepping out onto the moon. I heard on the radio about all the people getting killed in Vietnam for no reason, as far as I can tell. I read about Woodstock too, and heard about it on the radio. I sure would like to have been there. I can imagine what "out" looks like now, and I want to go there. I want to go home and live with my family. I want to finish school, get a motorcycle, and take Becka out on dates. Being here will only get harder after Nose leaves.

As Mr. Frybourne was deposing me, he began to take a personal interest in my case. Last week he contacted the judge and asked him to consider letting me go back home and get out patient therapy. I've hinted to Mr. Frybourne that I'll be a better witness on the stand if I'm free in the custody of my parents. You know, a bird in the bush sings better than a bird in the hand.

I'd like to think my story will end up being about something bigger than me. Maybe I won't know what it's about fully until after it ends. With Nose going home and Becka going home, I can't help but feel that the end for me will come soon.